# HARBIN'S RIDGE

# Harbin's Ridge

by
Henry and
Janice Holt Giles

Second Edition

HOUGHTON MIFFLIN COMPANY
BOSTON
1977

GPr SP

**Library of Congress Cataloging in Publication Data**

Giles, Henry E
    Harbin's Ridge.

    I. Giles, Janice Holt, joint author.    II. Title.
PZ4.G472Har5 [PS3513.I4626] 813'.5'4      76-47638
ISBN 0-395-25020-X

Printed in the United States of America
C   10   9   8   7   6   5   4   3   2   1

# Preface to the Second Edition

It was not intended as a hoax when *Harbin's Ridge* was originally published in Henry Giles' name alone. The book was actually written largely by me, Janice Holt Giles. But my husband had helped me so much with *The Enduring Hills* and would not allow me to use his name on that book, so I was determined when *Harbin's Ridge* was written he should have the credit; for as with *The Enduring Hills* he had furnished me with the idea. We are sorry to have deceived the public, but both my agent and publisher recognized my style of writing and knew the truth. So I don't feel too badly about it!

J. H. G.

C. 1

# one

T HIS IS MY LAST WILL AND TESTAMENT. A funny one, perhaps, since I've already divided what I've got among my children. I reckon this is more of a truth I'm leaving to the commonwealth. Whatever it is, I've a thing to tell. You're a writer. And a lawyer. That's why I sent for you. But don't go changing anything I say into something fine and fancy. Put it down just like I tell it. Good or bad that's the way it was, and that's the way I want it written down.

My name is Jeff Harbin. And I reckon if anybody could be said to know this old ridge of ours it would be me. For, man and boy, I've lived on it over sixty years. My folks have lived on it a sight longer than that. The first Harbin came to Kentucky with old Jim Harrod and Dan'l Boone, but when the wagons got to Crab Orchard where the trails forked, he took the Cumberland Trace instead of going on up to the settlements with them. He built him a cabin up here in the hills, cleared him a little patch of land and put him in a tobacco crop. There's been Harbins on this ridge ever since. That's why it's called Harbin's Ridge.

The ridge begins over at Pennyrile Hill, where the dirt road branches off the pike and crawls up out of the Green River bottoms. And it doglegs back and forth eight or ten miles down a hogback that humps itself up between Little Lost Creek on one side and the river on the other. This is the beginning of a chain of hills that ramble on down into Tennessee, getting higher and higher all the time until they join up with the Cumberland Mountains. They're called the Tennessee Hills hereabouts, on that account. But the part that's home to me is Harbin's Ridge and all the spurs and hollers that cut into it.

There's one right good-sized mountain at yon end of the ridge. It's called Lo and Behold. It's a sweet and curvey mountain, with its flanks set up against the sky. I don't rightly know how it came by its name, but the story goes that a traveling preacher in the old days was lost in these everlasting ridges and hollers. It had rained on him all the time and he couldn't get his direction day or night. He kept following the main ridge and finally when he came in sight of the mountain, lo and behold the sun broke through. It was said the whole top of the mountain was set afire with its glory, and the preacher got off his horse and knelt in the mud to give thanks to the Lord for showing him the way. That's as may be, but the mountain is called Lo and Behold to this day.

It's a good place to live, Harbin's Ridge. If you like to wake just as first light eases itself into the sky and cups the ridge with a thin, gray light. If you like to step outside your door in that milky grayness and watch it turn to mother-of-pearl, and then to a pink as soft as a young girl's blush. If you like to look down the head of the holler and watch the morning mists smoke up through the trees and listen while a cock crows the sun up over the farthest rim of the world. If you like to watch the first shafts of gold rub out the last stars of the night and dim the moon to a pale-riding ghost. If you like to stand while the gold spreads all over the sky and listen to a wood thrush drop his song like rippling water all around you. If you like to start your day soon, and no waste to it, the ridge will give you a morning like that to do it with.

And the end of the day is but its tucking away. It's a straight furrow plowed into the westering sun, the hours full-used, the animals fed and the night work done. It's the small glow of a lamp against the dark, and the warmth of a log on the fire against the cold. It's the settling up and the accounting of another turning of the earth.

And it's a good place if you like to have your own kind of folks all around you. I'd have to walk a far piece before I came across a man I didn't know. And I like the knowing of it. Friends and kinfolks all about, whether they're good or bad, makes a solid circle around a man . . . a circle that keeps strangeness out, and that keeps the known ways in. It's a friendly feeling to bound your land with neighbors and your own blood kin. It's like a piece of your own hearthfire was burning wherever you stop to pass the time of day.

Yes, it's a good place to live . . . Harbin's Ridge. If

your hands are curved to fit the handle of a plow and if your feet walk easy down a furrow. If you're the kind of man has got to push his head against the sky. And I reckon I'm that kind of man. For I wouldn't be able to breathe except there was a tall sky over me. And I wouldn't be able to rest at night without the trees and the land stretched about me.

Faleecy John was that kind of man, too. Only there was stronger tides of living inside him. As much as it's ever given one mortal to know another, I knew Faleecy John and those tides that pulled and tugged at him. For saving the three years my folks sent me outside to school, him and me was never apart. Like I know the ridge, I knew Faleecy John. The hills and hollers of his heart. The still places in his soul. The muddy, spurting streams of his wild blood. The big appetites and the greediness for life. I knew all of them, for he was closer to me than a brother, and I loved him better.

Faleecy John. Don't his name tell you the kind of man he was? Say it over soft-like two or three times. Faleecy John. Faleecy John. It's soft and it's hard. It's weak and it's strong. It's sand and it's rock. It's wine and it's water. Faleecy John. And he was all those things.

I've just to shut my eyes to see him now. Or maybe it's that I never get away from seeing him. He stood six foot four in his bare feet and his shoulders were so broad he had to angle to get through your door. His hands were like hams and he wore a size thirteen shoe. He had a head of rough black hair that sprang up like it had a life of its own, and the devil tended a fiery furnace in his eyes. A soot-black furnace that sparked a bright flame when he was pleased, or excited, or angry, and that scorched more than one girl who fluttered into their heat. He had a voice that roared like a bull when he was mad, but he could sing a ballad to his passing fancy and make it whisper like a lullaby. He'd give you the shirt off his back, and then lay your woman to warm him the minute you looked the other way. He was all hot or all cold. There wasn't any halfway between for Faleecy John. Not a minute of his life was he ever lukewarm.

But it's a long story and I'd better begin at the beginning. You understand I wasn't an eyewitness to everything I'm going to tell. That wouldn't be humanly possible. But what I didn't see and hear for myself I got from good report and I can vouch for the truth of it. When an old man starts looking back down the years he's apt to get a mite long-winded. I'll try not to do that. And you'll pardon me if I tell this my own way. I've had the schooling to know how to speak and write correctly. But a man talks easiest in his own tongue, and the speech of the hills comes natural to me.

However I tell it, it's all true, for there's not a twist or a turn of that long trail back down the years that I've forgot. You can't forget a man like Faleecy John, and I've more reason than most to remember.

# two

I<small>T WAS</small> my own grandma, my mother's ma, was the granny woman that cotched him the night he was born. And in a manner of speaking it was her gave him his name.

She had been a granny woman most of her days and had borned all the younguns up and down the ridge and in all the hollers in between. She'd go anywhere any time there was a need. They'd even come after her from over at Cherry Point, ten miles away. She had her a gentle old horse and a high-wheeled buggy, and night or day, rain or shine, when they come for her she took her little satchel, harnessed up her old horse, and went to help out.

She was good with the sick in all ways. Knew a heap

about herb medicines and doctoring. She knew that goldenseal, what we hereabouts call yaller-root, was good for stomach trouble, or sore mouth, or heart burn. She knew that flaxweed tea would cure the summer complaint in babies. She knew that goose grease was good to cut the mucous croup, and that ginseng would help chills and fever. She knew that sassafras tea was good to thin the blood and ward off biliousness, and that mullein boiled up and drunk hot would bring out the rash in chicken pox and measles. She knew a sight of things like that. As I look back on it I know that she was wiser than her time. She knew the ways of nature and she used her knowledge to help it along. She was cleaner than most, too, and the first thing she did, usual, when she went into a cabin was to fly in and redd things up and get the sick comfortable-like in a clean bed. She was a little trick of a person, but when she come through the door and started giving orders didn't nobody stand around arguing! But like I said, it was when a youngun was abirthing she was mostly needed.

It was a moony night in December when Ben Squires come after her. A full round moon was frozen in the sky, and the light lay cold and silver-still on the woods and fields, brittling them with a whiskering of rime. Even the wind lay quiet, unmoaning in the trees. Down in the holler a rutting fox barked hoarsely at the splintered stars and was quiet when they paid him no mind. A cow moved in the stall back in the barn and her bell tongued twice. The sound carried across the night, metal-strong and ringing, and then broke, shattered in the cold. The timbers in Granny's house shrank from the icy air and creaked as they drew into themselves. And when Ben Squires stepped up on the porch a loose board cracked under his foot like a whip being snapped. He knocked timid-like on the door.

When Granny opend to him he kept his eyes on his feet. "Lydie's time is on her," he said, and though he whispered, the words came rounded and clear in the cold.

Granny humphed and looked at him sharply. "You'd ort to be ashamed of yourself, Ben Squires," she said. "This is the tenth time you've come fer me in as many years. Looks like you could give that pore girl a rest!" She fanned the door wide. "Come in! Come in outen the cold! Don't jist stand there shiverin'. Hit'll take me a minnit. Git ye a cheer there by the fire. I've got to dress. When was she took?"

"About dusky dark was when she named it first." Ben hovered his hands over the coals in the fireplace.

"We'd best make time, then," and Granny bustled into the next room.

Granny lived on the main ridge, the one called Harbin's Ridge, and Ben lived on a spur that elbowed off down Raccoon Holler. Coming, he'd walked and cut across the holler. But driving they had to go plumb around the road, about two mile further. Ben rented over there on Hackberry Spur from old man Lockwood. Ben wasn't a pushing man and he'd never owned a piece of land of his own. He rented first one place and then another, but he'd been on old man Lockwood's place quite a spell then.

If you've never seen the kind of a house a man has to take when he rents on the ridge, commonly, I couldn't tell you so as you could understand. Ben's cabin wasn't much better than a barn, and not as good as a Harbin barn. It set in the middle of a clearing, away to hell and gone from neighbors and folks, and Granny always said why Lydie didn't die from pure lonesomeness was more than she could make out.

The cabin was just one room, made of logs, and most of the chinking had crumbled out long ago. Lydie kept the worst holes stuffed with old rags, but days when the wind mourned through the pines and drove the rain slashing ahead of it, the rags wasn't much help. The roof was made of shingleboards and in time it had been a good enough covering. But against the passing of the years the boards had weathered and curled. It leaked like a sieve and because the cabin wasn't ceiled you could lay on the straw pallet on the floor and look up and see the stars through the holes. I know, because I've done it more than once when I took the night with Faleecy John.

There was a rough board floor that buckled and sagged, with cracks between the boards wide enough that Lydie could sweep her trash through and never bother with opening her door. The hogs rooted under the house and the dogs slept there, and sometimes in the night they'd get to fighting and Ben'd grab him a fire log and pound the floor to make them quit.

It wasn't much of a place to live, I'll grant. The piney woods crept lonesome-like all about the cabin and kept the light and the sun from shining through. It was dark and damp, and many's the time I've had the feeling that Hackberry Spur stuck straight out over the edge of the world, lost and forgotten in time and space.

The Squireses cooked and ate and slept in that one room. They hadn't much to do with, either. Lydie cooked at the fireplace, and I never saw her use more than the spider, a long-handled skillet and an old iron kettle. If she had more, I never knew it. They had a table Ben had made out of new pine planks, set over against one wall, and when it seasoned one leg was shorter than the others and the table always rocked when you leaned your elbows on it. There was a bed in one corner. Of sorts. Ben had stuck a couple of poles in the logs and nailed them to a post at the corner. Lydie had taken some rope and crossed it back and forth and it held firm enough for them to lay their straw tick on. But Faleecy John never had a bed after he outgrew the cradle Ben made for their first one. He always slept on a straw pallet on the floor. Lydie would roll it up during the day and put it up on the beams overhead. Come night she'd get it down and spread it in the corner by the fire.

I've slept a many a night on that straw pallet with Faleecy John, and to two little fellows laying watching the fire, or looking up at the stars through the holes in the roof, it was as good a bed as could be found. I know now it was Faleecy John gave it all its magic. It was him could see castles in the flames, or reach up and pull the stars right through the roof. Once when he was pretending, he laughed low and excited-like and said, "See Jeffie! I've sprinkled stars all in your hair. It's all silver-shiney with light!" It wasn't but the night damp, where I'd been out under the pines, but Faleecy John could make it stars.

Some said that when Ben Squires was young he was a sightly lad, gaysome and peart, loving his banjo and a sprightly tune, and that Lydie was a sweet, light-stepping lass. But from the time I can recollect Ben was just a poor, shambling renter, picking his banjo in front of the fire on mournful winter nights, making him a little crop of corn and tobacco, and rambling the woods for a squirrel or a rabbit to help fill up the pot. Lydie still stood proud, and she'd borne the years better than Ben, but her body was gaunt and her face

was bitter, and when Ben started picking his banjo of a
winter night she never lifted her skirt to prance a light
step. Mostly she turned her face to the wall.

It was true that this was the tenth time in ten years
Ben had come to get Granny for Lydie. But hadn't a
one of the others lived. Mostly they didn't go their full
time, but if they did they were sad, blue little younguns
that never had a chance to live, and an hour or two was
about the best they could do.

That night when Granny got to Ben's cabin she
found it like she'd thought. Never once in all the times
she'd helped Lydie through a birthing did the woman
have so much as a bedsheet. When she was going to
Ben Squires' Granny always stuck a couple of clean
ones in her satchel, knowing she'd be needing them.

But she'd had Ben put on a kettle of water to heat, so
Granny set in and got Lydie and the bed all cleaned up,
and then she made herself a pot of strong coffee. She
allowed it would be anyhow the next morning before
the youngun come. Lydie always had a long, hard
time, and Granny figured this one would be like all
the rest.

But she hadn't much more than got herself set down
to her first cup of coffee when Lydie yelled a couple of
times, and before Granny could get across the room
that youngun was there! It mortally took her breath
away, seeing as Lydie had always taken so long before.
And it was a fine, healthy youngun, too. Granny
wrapped it in a blanket and saw to Lydie first.

"Is it dead?" Lydie asked when Granny tucked the
covers around her. Poor thing had got so used to all of
them being born dead.

"Cain't you hear it acryin'?" Granny said. "Hit's a
live, husky youngun this time!"

Lydie picked at the covers and the salt tears rolled

down her face. "Ten years hard-goin'," she said, "ten years of leetle dead babies. But I've got me a real live youngun at the end." And she raised up and pointed a bony finger at Ben who was roasting his rump over by the fireplace. "Fer it's the end, Ben Squires," she said, and the words came bitter and short. "You kin jist hang yore overhalls out in the woodshed, fer all of me. This un's the last! I ain't aimin' to tempt fate no more. And I'm aimin' to call it Faleecy, after my ma. I've had a yearnin' fer a leetle girl-child I could name Faleecy. All this time I've had sich a yearnin'."

"Hit's a boy," Granny said, not wasting any words.

Ben rubbed his hand over the stubble on his chin. "That bein' so," he said, "we'll name him John. After my pa."

Lydie set her mouth. "Girl or boy, hit's name is Faleecy."

"John."

"Faleecy!"

"John!"

They kept spitting them two names back and forth and Granny left them alone and went to settle the little fellow in his cradle. She unwrapped the blanket and looked him over good, and she said she never saw a finer boy-baby. Said he must of weighed nigh ten pounds. Had a chest on him like a barrel, fat, chunky legs and arms, and a round little bottom as plump as a partridge. And because it pleasured her so to see such a fine, healthy youngun, and because of pure loving him so good, Granny hoisted him high 'up over her head. Naked as a bluejay she lifted him up and shook him, she was that pleased with him. Lydie and Ben was still spitting at one another.

"Faleecy," Lydie'd say.

"John," Ben'd snap right back.

Granny laughed. "Well, now! Faleecy John!" she said. "That's a right nice name for so peart a youngun. Faleecy John! I don't know as I ever heared a nicer one."

She gave him one last shake, high over her head, and that little boy-baby bowed his back, arched his belly, stiffened his legs, and let loose a shower, plumb in Granny's face! To her dying day Granny loved to tell about it. And to the time he was a man grown she'd tease Faleecy John about it. "Faleecy John," she'd call out to him, it made no differ where, "Faleecy John, you learnt to hold yer water yit?" And then she'd cackle in high glee.

When he was a little fellow it mortified him plumb to death, but when he got bigger he'd come right back at her. "Why, Granny," he'd say, "how was I to know yore wrinkled old face from the trunk of a tree!"

But that was how Faleecy John come by his name. And none ever suited a man better.

# three

I T WAS a little better than two years later, on a moony night in June instead of December, that Papa went after Granny to help birth me. Granny laughed at how scared he was. Said he was shaking like he had the ague. She always allowed the old ones was a heap scareder than the young ones. Not that Papa was old, mind. But thirty-six can't be counted first youth anywheres. And it's getting on for a man on the ridge to be whelping his first one. Commonly we marry young.

My mother was just past sixteen, though, when I was born. Even these days the girls marry young here on the ridge, but in the old days a girl wasn't likely to let her fifteenth birthday creep up on her without being wedded. And Lucibel hadn't. She'd been married at fifteen, and like I said, I was born when she'd just turned sixteen. Papa was twenty years older than her.

I asked Granny one time, when I was up pretty good-sized, why Papa waited so long to marry, and she just lipped her snuff and looked wise and said a burnt child dreads the fire. So I reckoned there must of been some truth in the tale that he'd loved once before and lost his love to another man.

But Granny never minded telling how he courted my mother. How he used to come of a Saturday night all spruced and slicked, his black hair brushed flat and his face sweet-smelling and clean from shaving. And how his mare was always curried and combed, too. She'd laugh when she'd tell how mad he used to get when there was other young fellows hanging around, and how when Lucibel went to a shindig with one of them one Saturday night he drooped by the fire and put his head in his hands and told Granny he'd just about despaired of her ever taking notice of him, and that he couldn't say as he faulted her, her being just turned fifteen and him so much older. "It's likely," he'd said, and his voice was hollow with sadness, "she'd ought to take one younger and more in keeping with her own years."

But Granny had laughed at him and told him faint heart never won fair lady. She never made any bones about favoring him over the others, and not even to his face did I ever know her to deny her reasons. She said it would be a poor out of a mother didn't want her own daughter to marry well, and there was no gainsaying Papa had right smart land and a good, tight house. On top of that he was a fine figure of a man, standing tall and broad and handsome, with his hair like a crow's wing and his eyes to match. It always grieved me that I never took after him.

Granny said it would never be her advice to any girl

to marry for what a man had laid by, but it was past her understanding why if a man had stored up considerable and was likely-looking to boot, a girl couldn't pull a little on the reins in his direction. It didn't signify she was marrying him for what he had at all. It just added up to plain common sense.

She must of heartened Papa considerably, for when he went the next Saturday night he made bold to ask Lucibel for her hand straight out, and the way Granny tells it, they never wasted any time getting to the preacher's.

Papa used to tease Granny about feathering her own nest, but none could claim she had that in mind. For she never lived a minute under Papa's roof, and right to the last she made her little garden patch, did her grannying, and went her own way. But she liked Papa, and she took pride in Lucibel being his woman.

There in that old room across the hall was where she spanked the life into me that June night sixty-five years ago. And it's not much changed since that night. This has been a Harbin house for twice sixty-five years. It came to me from my father, who had it from his father before him.

I've always had a fondness for the way this house sits off the road the way it does, spread out rambling and sprawling under the chestnut oaks. It rambles and sprawls because we've all added to it, and there never has been any rhyme or reason to the way the rooms have been added. Grandpa built the first house and it was just two log rooms with the dogtrot in between. He angled an ell off in the back before he died, and then Papa closed in the dogtrot and made it a hall, and put an upstairs over the whole thing. In my turn I built two rooms to the side of the ell and put porches all around. It's a rambling, sprawling old house, all right. But it's tight-built and sturdy. When the wind blows cold across the ridge of a winter's night there's never a quake or a shake in the whole enduring house. It hunkers around the fireplaces solid and stout, and hovers a snug shelter over all that's within. Summers, with the hall doors folded back and the windows thrown wide, there's always a fan of breeze playing through the rooms. It's a house built for comfort and for family living. It's known its share of grief and heartache, but it's known its joy and laughter, too.

I like to step out on the back porch and look across what's mine. Most any man takes pleasure in his own. There to the right are the orchards. Peach and apple and pear, all growing together, and clover bedded down beneath.

Straight back is Ida's garden patch, with her pretties hemming it in. She's a great hand for flowers. Just as likely as not to plant March roses alongside the onions. It's a fair sight to see come summer, her garden is. Green beans rambling up the poles, squash yellowing on the vines, tomatoes hanging round and red and heavy, bending the plants almost to the ground. And all around and in between Ida's flowers, pretty as a picture and smelling up the air.

On back of the garden is the tobacco patch, and back of it is the upper pasture. From that highest spot in the pasture you can look off down the holler through the gap in the hills and see five miles of Little Lost Creek winding and twisting in the valley. Unless the mists are hanging low, that is, and then the holler looks like a box of smoke, and the gap is hid from sight.

Off there to the left are the barns. The big tobacco barns, and the stock barn, and the hay barn, with the old rail fence closing them in. The whole place is fenced with rails. The barn lots, the orchards, the house yard and the fields. My boy Jeff will take down the old rail fences when the place comes to him. He's got no patience with the old ways, nor much of an eye for beauty. He says wire is best. Maybe so. But I like the feel of a rail fence under my hand, and I like the line of it curving over the lay of the land, and I like the gray look of it in the rain. Old gray things, fences, houses or barns, have a look of time about them. A softness, like the years had slipped easy over them. In my time I'll have no wire fences.

It's untelling the times me and Faleecy John have walked the snake-back of that barnyard fence. It was always him that give the dare. "I kin walk the furthest without fallin' off!" he'd yell. And usual, he did.

But I mind the time he come to grief. He was seven, I reckon, and I was five. It was one of those hot days that come in a long, dry spell in July sometimes. When the sun rides the sky like a ball of fire the whole day long, and the heat presses down and the earth soaks it up and gives it back in a shimmer like steam from scalded sheet-iron. When the leaves on the chestnut oaks hang tired and thirsty, and the cows stand knee-deep, unmoving, in the ponds.

We had been playing in the hay barn, but the hay was hot and dusty and it got inside our shirts and mixed with our sweat and made us itch. We wandered outside and Faleecy John squatted down beside the barn on his heels like he'd seen the menfolks do, and picked him a stalk of hay to chew on. I stood and made marks in the dust with my bare toes.

"What kin we do next?" he asked. Faleecy John was never one to be still for very long.

"We kin climb the big apple tree," I said.

He shook his head. "We done that yesterday."

"We kin fish in the pond," I offered next.

He was scornful. He knew that my mother wouldn't let me go down to the creek to fish. But sometimes we'd pretend we were catching fish in the pond. Days when he felt like pretending, it was a lot of fun. We'd made us a raft out of old planks and we'd pole it out in the middle of the pond and dangle our legs in the water and see who could catch the most pretend fish. But today was one of his bigger days, and he was head and shoulders above pretending. "Ain't no fish in that leetle old pond," he said. And I turned red for having mentioned it. It was like I had betrayed his bigness.

Desperately I culled my mind to think of something. I was afraid he'd go home if I didn't think of something extra special. He did sometimes. Right in the middle of the most fun he'd start loping across the meadow. "I gotta go," he'd say, and I would stand and watch him getting smaller and smaller in the distance, and my own heart would get small inside of me until it was like it had gone with Faleecy John and left me empty and crying. I had always that lonely, bereft feeling when he went away from me, like a bleeding when a part of yourself is cut off. But even then I knew it was no use begging him to stay. Faleecy John would only give you as much of himself as he wanted.

So in sudden anguish I thought of the rail fence. I was scared to walk the rail fence. I had fallen too often, and I knew I always would. I was afraid of falling from the minute I climbed up on it, and I took every step with fear dogging my heels. It was always something of a relief when I finally toppled off and Faleecy John could hop around on one foot and crow over me, "I beat! I beat! I didn't fall!" I could brush myself off and limp on to the next game, putting the rail fence once more behind me.

I stood there torn between the two fears . . . walking the rail fence or losing Faleecy John. Faleecy John loved to walk the fence. He would run, with all the carelessness of seven, fleetly and surely along the rail, his feet white and swift on the gray wood. His black head would shine in the sun and he would laugh, high and shrill. "Come on, Jeffie! Hurry! If you stop you'll fall!"

But I, clumsy and awkward, and always afraid, would inch slowy behind, the ground swimming up at me. Inevitably there would come that hesitant moment when I would teeter, and the fear would swallow me up whole, and I was lost. "Oh Jeffie," Faleecy John would say, "you've got to run fast, Jeffie. You've got to git started an' then keep goin', and don't look at the ground. Jist keep goin', Jeffie." But how could I keep going when I could never get started!

"We could walk the rail fence," I said slowly. Deliberately I could offer myself up to that fear in sacrifice to the other and greater. I drew another mark in the dust with my toe and hoped, hopelessly, that Faleecy John would reject this offering, too. Hoped, and feared, until my breath was tight in my chest, that this might be too small a gift to lay before him.

Like a rabbit raising a dust down the road he was off across the barn lot. "Let's see kin we walk clean around the barn," he screamed, clambering up on the rails, "clean around the barn, Jeffie! I bet I kin! I bet I kin!" Already his toes were gripping the rail and his heels had wings. My own were heavy with fear, but there was a lightness inside that lifted me up. Faleecy John wouldn't go home for a while!

At the first rider he paused. "First one falls off is a
. . . " he stopped to think. Sometimes it was a yaller-
bellied hound dog. Sometimes it was a ring-tail coon.
Sometimes it was a rotten egg. I waited, watching him
work his mind over various epithets. He scanned the
sky and the countryside and then his eyes fell to the
ground. "First one falls off is," he yelled triumphantly,
scrambling over the rider, "is a piece of chicken shit!"

The words knifed through me and left a wide,
wounded hole. It would be me, I knew, and Faleecy
John had consigned me to the final and most awful
humiliation. Nothing was so small, so hopelessly trivial,
so ultimately worthless! If he had just said cow stuff,
now. At least that made a sizeable pile, and could be
spread over the fields to make things grow. But chicken!
That's what Papa called anything low-down, trifling,
no-good!

And the wickedness in his black eyes when he slanted
a look at me told me Faleecy John had deliberately
named it to shame me. That was what I couldn't bear!
A lump clawed its way up into my throat and knotted
there, and I was afraid I was going to cry. I ducked my
head and swallowed down the lump. Beggar though I
was for Faleecy John's favor, I had my own kind of
pride. I wouldn't let him know I minded at all. Not
that I hoped pride would keep me on the fence longer
than him. I knew it wouldn't. But I could pretend
what he'd named was no worse than yaller-bellied
hound dog. So I made my eyes blink the shine away
and followed him carefully across the rider.

Faleecy John had got about halfway around the barn
and I was inching along three or four lengths behind
when it happened. You know how a snake-rail fence
is built. Zigzag. Every time it zigs or zags it makes a
corner, and a long rail was propped on either side at

every corner to strengthen the fence. These slanted
rails are called riders. There was an extra-long rider just
yon side the barn. Faleecy John was hitting his stride,
leapfrogging the riders as they came, when he came up
to that long one. I'd just made the turn and looked up
in time to see him slide across. And then I saw him
jerk and hang there in midair. His britches had hung
on a spike and yanked him clean off his feet.

He started yelling and kicking, but he was hung
good and proper, and his overhalls being new was too
stout to give. I crawled down and ran as fast as I could
to help him. But he looked so funny hanging there, his
feet kicking, and his shoulders twisting and turning,
and his face red with madness, that I couldn't help but
laugh. It commenced with a giggle and got mixed up
with the lump I hadn't hardly swallowed yet and ended
up with me howling until I rolled in the dust. Which
only made Faleecy John madder.

"Git me loose!" he yelled, and he beat at me with his
fists. "Git me down from here, goddammit to hell!
Sunavabitch! Jeffie!" And then that final epithet,
"Chicken shit! You git me down from here! I'll kill
you, Jeffie! I'll kill you if you laugh at me! Git me
down!"

Sobered, I crawled up on the fence beside him and
tried to loose him. But he wouldn't be still, and even
if he had it needed the weight lifted off the spike to
free him. He was still cussing blue blazes, naming every
foul thing he'd ever heard his pa say, when Lucibel
came flying into the lot, her skirts whirling the dust
ahead of her.

I wish I could tell you about my mother so that you
could see her as she was then. There's a picture of her
over the mantel in the front parlor taken along about

that time. A photographer passed this way one day, and Papa had him take it. He did the best he could, and it favors her a heap, but no picture could ever do her justice. You had to see her eyes sparkling, and her mouth dimpling, and you had to hear her laugh rippling, and her voice singing, and you had to watch her moving, like a willow in a wind, to really see her. No picture could catch the life of her.

Her hair was yellow, like the butter her hands patted out, and her eyes were greeny-gold, like the water down in Little Lost Creek. She was little and slim and sweet, and she was given to singing and laughter and gayness. She was a lovesome thing, and she was as good as she was pretty. I thought then, and I do now, that she was the best and the most beautiful woman in the world.

I never called her Mama. Papa called her Lucibel and I reckon I picked it up from him. Once when he was scolding me about it Lucibel made him quit. "I like it," she said, "and it's me he's calling. Leave him be." No more was ever said about it, and she was Lucibel to me all her life.

She came storming into the barn lot, her mouth set and the freckles on her nose shining against the whiteness of her face. "Shut up!" she said to Faleecy John, her voice low like it always was, but the words coming sharp and temper-edged. "Shut up this very minute! What do you mean, Faleecy John Squires? Talking like that! The very idea!"

Faleecy John shut up, but his eyes shot lightning at her. "Git me down," he said fiercely.

"I'll get you down," she said, "but if I ever hear another word like that out of you, you'll never step foot on Harbin land again. You hear!" She went up close to him and shook his leg. "You hear me!"

Faleecy John nodded and then she climbed up on the rail beside him and set to work getting him loose. It took her quite a time, him being a solid-built boy and her being scant-weighed herself, but she finally had him free and they crawled down the fence together.

Then Faleecy John, being but a little boy for all his fierceness, crumpled in the dust and went to crying. Not for hurt, nor for fear lived through, but for mortification and lost pride and for shame that he had to take a woman's help. Like it had been my own, I felt it run through me, and my tears of grief joined his in the dust. Lucibel knelt beside us, her skirts spread fanwise in the dirt, and gathered us close.

"There," she said softly, snuggling us each against a shoulder, "now, there! No call to cry. No harm's been done. Faleecy John's got a snag in his overhalls and maybe a splinter in his skin, but what's that to cry about? Hush, now. Hush, It's all right."

And like a salve spread on a flaming burn, peace laid over us and soothed the fire of grief. Faleecy John snuffed and turned his cheek against her throat. And then I felt the arm holding me jerk suddenly. She pushed us both away and her hand flew to her neck. She stared at Faleecy John and a scarlet tide flowed up into her face. He swayed toward her gently, and his head dropped before her look, but a smile quivered sweetly at the corners of his mouth.

A moment longer she knelt, looking at him and then she stood brusquely, sweeping her skirts about her. The scarlet had gone from her face now, leaving it naked and still. Then she laughed and held out a hand to each of us. "Come," she said, her voice trilling a singing tone, "there's a big, fat watermelon cooling in the spring. Let's cut it and see if it's ripe." And we raced to the spring house, Lucibel beating us both.

We ate that whole big watermelon, just the two of us, for Lucibel said she didn't believe she wanted any after all and went on in the house. I ate two long slices myself, and Faleecy John ate the rest. He stuffed and he stuffed and he kept on stuffing himself with watermelon, and I watched him wondering where he could put it all. He didn't want the last of it, either. But he ate it when he found out Papa would throw it to the hogs. He looked at it and then he sighed. "It's too good to waste," he said and he crammed it down. I thought it was funny that he'd rather eat something he didn't want than to let it get away from him.

I went piece the way home with him, then, trying thus to stave off that inevitable moment when I must stand, left behind, and watch him smalling in the distance. Slowly we went down the road, I, in exquisite pain, squeezing the last joy from the day. It was a long piece down the road yet to the bend. You could hardly see it from the gate. That much farther I could go. That much longer I could possess Faleecy John.

We spatted our feet in the hot dust and squiggled it up between our toes. We cut sassafras switches with Faleecy John's big knife and tickled the fuzzy caterpillars crawling in the shade. And then we turned the switches into stick horses and galloped a leaf-swept trail down the road. We found some late blackberries in a fence corner and ate them. Not being very hungry we only ate a few. Then we crushed the rest and stained our hands. There was enough to go clear up to our wrists.

We dallied and spun out the time, but the bend of the road came closer and closer, and at last we stood in the place and the time beyond which I could not go. I turned. This time I would not watch him go. The familiar sinking feeling turned with me, but I would not let myself look back. How brave one can be at five!

Then a high, sweet, piercing whistle shrilled over me, and Faleecy John was laughing by my side. "Here," he said, holding out his hand. "I made it fer you. You've been wantin' a reed whistle. I brung it to you today. Hit's on account of we're friends." And his smile broke sweet and sunny over his face.

We were eating supper that night when Papa looked at Lucibel and a frown puckered his face. "Why, Lucibel," he said, "what's the matter with your throat? Looks like something's bit you!" He reached his hand out and touched a red mark lying dark against the whiteness of her neck. When he took his hand away I could see the bruises, looking like small tooth prints.

Lucibel smiled. "Something did," she said, " a small wild thing I was trying to gentle."

Papa shook his head. "There's no gentling small wild things, Lucibel. They'll be docile for a time, but it's not their nature to be tamed. Best leave them wild, like they're born to be."

My heart was thudding hard against my side. Something was being said I didn't understand. Something had been done I didn't understand. And it frightened me and I didn't like it. My reed whistle was cool and slick in my pocket against my hand. I brought it forth and laid it on the table, and defiantly I said, "See what Faleecy John made me." I said it loudly so no one could mistake. "Faleecy John made me a whistle. On account of we're friends!"

# four

STARTED to school in July after my sixth birthday in June. Lucibel didn't much want me to start so soon. I remember she cried and said I was too little to be going off from her. But Papa said the time was so short I'd better go as soon as I could.

The school term here on the ridge is only seven months long at best, and sometimes it has to be cut to six. It takes up the second Monday in July. There's never any question about that. But how late it goes depends on the weather. Comes a hard winter with lots of rain and frost, it closes in January. The roads get too bad and the building can't be kept warm and folks won't send their younguns out. Of a mild winter it runs on into February, but never later than that.

That was the way it was in my day, and it hasn't changed much in fifty years. The younguns still go down the holler to the same little white frame building for six or seven months out of the year, just like I did. It's in my mind that the teacher still takes up books with the same old cracked dinner bell, and I reckon if you want to look you'll find my mark on more than one of the desks. The ridge is slow to change. Most times I hold with that. It pays to ponder a thing before making a move. But fifty years is long enough to ponder and the school needs changing a heap.

Faleecy John came by for me early that morning, and Lucibel went to the gate with us. I had on a new pair of overhalls and a checked gingham shirt she'd made for me and my hair was wetted and slicked down in place. No amount of wishing could make it black like Faleecy John's. Nothing could change its sandy lankness. But at least I had it plastered every hair in place. Lucibel laughed a little when she saw how I had it slicked down and she ran her hand over it, roughing it. I pulled away. "Don't," I said impatiently. I wondered that she couldn't tell I was too big, now, for her to make over. Six years old and going to school! Anybody should know that was might near growed up! But Lucibel's mouth was quirked down at the corners and I was afraid she would shame my importance in front of Faleecy John by crying again. She might even kiss me! So I grabbed my dinner bucket from her hand and put the gate between us.

"See to him," she said to Faleecy John, and my pride shuffled the dust under my feet. See to him! Gall flowed sour under my tongue. Bitterly I kicked at a rock beside the road. It rolled over and exposed a fat, bleached grub which stretched and squirmed uneasily. I set my heel on it and twisted hard and the grub split and its insides spread over my heel. The feel of the soft slimy stuff gave me a chill up my back, but it also restored something of my bigness. Power and importance came back to me and I marched off down the road, standing tall and striding long, and I never once looked back.

It was a sweet morning, bright with sun but not yet laid over heavy with heat. Books took up at eight o'clock, and we had a three-mile walk, so it was only nearing seven when we started out. The dust in the road was damped down by the dew and it felt cool and moist under our feet. There was a little wind blowing and when we passed under the trees it sent a small shower down on us, and we stood and held our faces up and let it sprinkle on them. Faleecy John stuck his tongue out to see what dew tasted like. But he said it was so scant he couldn't tell.

The tobacco was waist-high in the patches by the fence rows, its broad green leaves misted over with dew-frosting. It was just coming on to bloom, and when you looked out across a whole field of it, it looked like a pale lilac sea. Faleecy John hated tobacco with a passion, for he had to help with the whole enduring crop, from setting out to stripping and bulking down. But even he had to admit it was a sightly thing to look upon when it was in bloom. Lilac, lavender, amethyst, I don't rightly know the color of it. But Granny had a plant in an old churn she tended once that had a bloom for all the world like it. She called it an oleander. This morning the blooms stood up tall and proud, and when they bent in the wind the sun caught a million sparkling diamonds in their cups.

When we turned down the path through the holler it was laced across with hundreds of spider webs. Their

patterns were beaded with dew and splashed with all
the colors of the rainbows. We went around to keep
from breaking them. Besides, they're a nuisance to get
in your hair.

We saw three lizards sunning on a rock, and an old
king snake creeping along by the brook. We threw
stones at him, but we didn't really try to hit him, for
king snakes are good to keep the poison snakes away.
It's true that if a king snake stays around your place no
poison snake will come. Faleecy John told me about a
man once watched a king snake and a rattlesnake have a
fight. The rattlesnake would bite the old king snake
and he'd crawl off and eat some sort of grass was growing close by and then go back and fight some more.
He'd wrap himself around the rattler and squeeze tight,
and when the rattler bit him again he'd crawl off and
eat grass. Finally he wore the rattlesnake down to
where he just squeezed the life out of him.

It was a fine morning to be starting to school, and I
felt high and handsome and mighty proud.

It was a funny thing, though. When we came in sight
of the schoolhouse I thought of Lucibel standing at the
gate, and I wished I could go back. I wished I'd let her
rumple my hair, and I even wished I'd kissed her good-
bye. The closer we got the more I thought of her, and
the power and the importance ebbed away until I felt
no bigger than the grub I'd squashed. My heart kept
swelling in my chest and my breath kept getting shorter
until I didn't know but what I was maybe going to die.

And when I was sick by the side of the road and lost
my breakfast I knew I was going to die, and I thought
how tight Lucibel's arms could hold you, and how soft
her voice could sing to you, and how sweet and clean
she always smelled. And I thought how she would cry

if I should die so far away from her, way down here in the holler by the side of the road. It made a big lump in my throat and when I'd finished being sick I told Faleecy John, "I think I'll go home."

Faleecy John wiped my face with my shirttail and then he tucked it back inside my overhalls carefully. He picked up my dinner bucket and handed it to me. And then he took me by the hand. "You cain't," he said, matter of factly, "you gotta go to school. I'll see to you." And he led me on down the road.

See to me! There was a mort of comfort in those words, now. And the feel of Faleecy John's hard, thin hand was a rod and a staff. He didn't turn loose of my hand until books took up, and then he seated me beside him at his desk. I was still feeling fluttery and a little sick, and wondering how a body could stand seven long months of school, when the teacher started taking down the names of the new pupils. When he came to me such an agony of embarrassment took hold of me that I couldn't speak. I tried, but I couldn't make the words come out, and finally when the kids started tittering and laughing I just scrooched down in the seat and tried to hide behind Faleecy John's shoulder. He nudged me and made me sit up. "All you got to do is tell him yer name," he whispered fiercely. "Jist say yer name!"

I was just about to manage it when a little girl across the aisle, a pretty little girl with yellow braids hanging down her back, stuck her tongue out at me and crossed her eyes and hissed so everybody could hear, "Cat's got yer tongue! Cat's got yer tongue!"

Mortified to pieces and feeling lashed and torn by this strange and cruel new world I slunk down in the seat again, and the fluttery sickness welled up once more. I hid my face against Faleecy John and shuddered. And then the dam broke and the tears flowed. Faleecy John put his arm about my shoulders. "His name is Jeff Harbin," he told the teacher, and his voice was strong and sure in my ears.

He didn't try to make me sit up again. He just sat still and steady with his arm around my shoulder, and every once in a while his hand would pat, not soft and gentle like Lucibel's, but easy and careless-like, more like the way Papa's hand would touch the bay mare's colt. When I finally snubbed the tears away and sat up he got out his pencil and tablet and drew me some pictures. And then he gave over the pencil and tablet to me and told me I could draw.

By recess time I felt a lot better, but it all came back a heap worse when we went outside to play. The little girl started it by giggling and pointing her finger. "Crybaby," she said, and she made like a little baby crying. "Crybaby!" and then she hopped around on one foot, laughing and wrinkling up her nose. "Cat's got his tongue!" she mocked and giggled, "cat's got his tongue, an' he's a crybaby!"

Another little girl standing close by cried, "Shame on you, Jolie!" But the other kids had already taken it up, and there was a ring of them forming around me and Faleecy John, all laughing and mocking and calling, "Cat's got his tongue!"

One of the biggest boys was the worst, and he kept inching in from the circle until finally he poked me in the side, "Yah, yah!" he cried, "mama baby! Little Jeffie Harbin's a mama baby! Got to have somebody look after him! Got to have Faleecy John look after him! Does Faleecy John fix you a sugar tit when you cry, little baby?"

Quicker than I ever saw him move Faleecy John was

on top of him and the two of them went down and rolled in the dust. When they stopped rolling Faleecy John was on top, and he straddled the other one and started pounding him with both fists. Before the teacher could get there he had busted out two teeth for the boy and closed one eye. I never knew he could get so mad! He was just like a wildcat turned loose. Even when the Combs boy started yelling quits Faleecy John kept on pounding him, his face as white as chalk and his teeth biting into his lip. The teacher and some of the other boys had to drag him off, and he still kept flailing away, clawing and scratching at all of them. The teacher shook him hard to bring him to his senses. "What are you trying to do, boy, kill him?"

Faleecy John stood there and the way he was trembling was plain for all to see. He shook his head and pushed his hair back out of his eyes. But he never said a word. Just his eyes kept on hating the Combs boy who was over under the tree spitting out his teeth. The teacher shook Faleecy John again. "A fight's a fight, Faleecy John, but Estil was calling quits. You don't hit a guy after he calls quits, don't you know that?"

"I never heared him," Faleecy John mumbled.

The teacher grunted and walked over to see what he could do for Estil Combs. Which wasn't much, seeing his teeth were gone and his eye was closed fast. "The next one fights on the school ground will have me to lick," the teacher said, and he rung the bell for books.

When Faleecy John and I reached the gate that evening Lucibel was waiting. Just like she hadn't left all day. She put her hands behind her when she saw us coming and she laughed and made a little crowing sound in her throat like she sometimes did when she was pleased. "Guess, and you can have them," she said, backing off from us and hiding her hands.

We guessed cookies, and she shook her head.

We guessed apples, and she shook her head.

We guessed watermelon, and she shook her head.

Finally she looked sad and said, "Well, shucks! I reckon I'll just have to eat them myself," and she brought out two fried peach pies! Nobody could make fried pies like Lucibel. They were flaky and crusty and dusted over with sugar, and they fairly melted in your mouth. She held them up and we grabbed for them, and knowing we were hungry she didn't tease us long. She sat down in the grass with us and spread her skirts down to her ankles. When she was fixed just so she rumpled my hair and I leaned against her, not caring a bit to be made over. "And how was school today?" she asked, pulling Faleecy John up close on the other side.

Faleecy John swallowed his pie. "Fine," he said, "jist fine. Jeffie made out all right. He done good."

Not a word about me being sick! Not a word about me crying! Not a word about him having a fight on account of Estil Combs calling me a mama baby! Just fine, he said, and it was like his hand was on my shoulder again. It was me and Faleecy John being two growed men, keeping our business to ourselves, and not bothering our womenfolks with it. We could make out for ourselves. Lucibel was soft and sweet to lean against, and we thanked her for the fried pies. But we had our own affairs, me and Faleecy John, and Lucibel wouldn't understand the way of them.

# five

T HE NEXT morning I didn't want to go to school. I had no illusions now about it, nothing like pride and importance to uphold me. I knew what school was like, and I didn't want any more of it. But I couldn't say so, after Faleecy John had said I got along so good. So I made out like I felt sick, which I did too much for comfort, thinking Lucibel wouldn't make me go then.

I didn't eat much breakfast and she and Papa both got a worried look and Lucibel said maybe I was coming down with something. Papa said it could be and maybe I should stay home today. Then he went out to the barn to feed. I drooped around and Lucibel commenced redding up the dishes, eyeing me every once in a while. "You hurt anywhere, Jeffie?" she asked.

35

"No'm," I mournfully answered, "I just don't feel good."

"You're not hot," she fretted, "likely it's just something you've eat."

"Likely," I agreed.

Then Papa came back to the house, excited and hurrying. "The brindle cow's dropped a heifer calf," he said, and I forgot I was feeling sick and ran out to the barn to see. Papa let me rub its soft, wet nose, and then he told me to go to the house and get some clean rags. When I went running into the kitchen, yelling at the top of my voice, Lucibel was packing my dinner bucket, and her mouth was set in a straight line. She never said a word, just handed me the lard pail she'd packed my dinner in, and I took it and went slowly to the gate to wait for Faleecy John. Lucibel was sure hard to fool!

When I looked back she was taking the clean rags out to the barn to Papa herself. And I knew that I *had* to go to school. Not just today, but every day for seven long months. And not just seven months this year, but seven months every year, year after year, until I was through. And the time stretched out ahead of me long and endless, and I thought all the fun of life was over.

But that very day I began to like it better. The teacher gave me a seat of my own and a first reader and I started to learn my A B C's. When I stood by the teacher's desk that afternoon and spelled out the letters of my first word, a whole new world was opened to me. A whole wide world of words and writing and the limitless horizon of books. Even then I knew a prickle of excitement and it edged into my voice. When I lifted my eyes from the page and looked at the teacher there was a strangeness on his face and he held my look for a long time. "Well," he said, "well, Jeff Harbin!" and the prickle ran all over me and made me trembly in my knees. That teacher was Rafe Smollet, as good a teacher as ever lived. He knew already that here before him was aborning another lover of books.

Faleecy John could never understand why I loved books so much. He was quick to learn, far quicker than I. But he had no patience with it. It was like he learned quickly to have it over and done with. Books had no charm for him. He was glad to close their covers, and he was always the first one out the door when the teacher called, "Books away!" at the end of the day.

Later, when we were older, he'd sometimes come when I was deep in reading. And he'd snatch my book and run away with it. "Don't bury yerself in a old book, Jeffie," he'd say. "Look! The sun's ashinin'! The fish are bitin' in the beaver hole! It's too good to waste, Jeffie! It's too good to waste!" And I'd forget my book for a time and we'd go fishing.

That day, too, I learned that the little girl with the yellow braids was named Jolie Turner and that she lived down on Little Lost Creek. She gave me a raisin cookie from her dinner pail, and I forgot that she called me cry baby.

The girl who had cried "Shame" when the kids were teasing the day before gave me a cookie, too. She had straight, plain brown hair, and there were freckles on her nose. Her name was Ida Stone. But I didn't ask where she lived.

Oh yes. By and large I liked school a heap better after the second day. And the first week flew by and come Friday I wasn't minding going at all. Fact is, I was wondering how I'd ever passed the time before I went to school. It seemed like a long way back to re-

member when I was just a little, little boy with un-
numbered hours to wander the orchard and the pasture
and the barn lot in. All the power and all the importance had come to stay, and I didn't think much of anything could ever happen now to scare them away.

But something did. For that Friday evening when
Faleecy John and I come out into the wide clearing at
the head of the holler on our way home from school he
laid his books down on the edge of the grass. "Put yore'n
down," he said, and I did, wondering. "You got to
learn to fight," he said, and his voice was level and
even, and his face was flat and quiet.

"What for?" I said.

"You got to learn to stand up fer yerself, Jeffie, an'
I'm goin' to learn you so's won't nobody never lick
you," and his fist shot out and knocked me flat. He
came over and helped me up. "That's the first thing fer
you to learn," he said. "Don't never stand waitin' fer
a feller to make the first move. Don't stand there easy-
like, trustin' him. He'll take you by surprise if you
do." And his fist shot out again.

This time he let me pick myself up. The surprise
and the hurt were passing in me and I was getting mad.
Twice he'd knocked me down when I was listening.
All right, I'd quit listening, and I went at him fast, my
arms windmilling the air. He knocked me flat again.
"You'll waste yerself thataway," he said when I rolled
over. "Double up yer fists an' hit from yer heels."

He circled and waited while I crawled back up, and
I doubled my hands into fists and circled with him.
When we closed again I got in two or three good
punches before he knocked me down. "That's better,"
he grunted, "you got in a good un then. That there'n
to my stummick. Aim fer the stummick or the jaw."

I pulled myself up and we circled again. I felt sore
and shaken and my head was beginning to ache. My
mouth was cut, too, and when I ran my tongue over
it I tasted blood. "Can't you teach me the rest tomorrow?" I asked.

"We'll quit when you've knocked me down oncet,"
he said, and I landed on my back again. I lay there and
shut my eyes and the stones of the clearing bit into my
back. I wanted to cry and a whimper came up into my
throat. "If you cry, Jeffie," Faleecy John threatened,
"I'll black both yer eyes and knock all yer teeth out!"

And I knew he would.

I turned over and pushed myself up with my hands
and knees and the trees that rimmed the clearing rocked
in front of me. "I can't," I said to myself. "I can't
knock him down." I didn't know I'd said it out loud
until I heard his voice, relentless and grim, "You got to
Jeffie. You got to!"

He kept knocking me down and I kept getting up
and I lost count of the times. Whatever anger I felt
at first got used up and all I could feel was weariness
and hopelessness. He'd knock me down and I'd get up.
But I got up. Even at the last when he was just a
moving blur in front of me, I kept getting up, and I
kept trying to knock him down so I could rest. Sometimes I'd get two or three good ones in, sometimes I'd
just pick myself up and go back down. But what my
wearied mind didn't understand was that Faleecy John
wasn't much bigger than me, and that if I was so tired
I could hardly stand, he was getting awfully tired, too.
He was a mighty little fellow to be teaching anybody
how to fight!

I reckon he finally ran into one that rolled him over.
I didn't remember punching him, but he went down

and I stood there and rocked over him, and then I lay down beside him and laid my arm across him. I was so glad not to have to get up again! And I reckon he was glad, too. We just laid there, heaving and panting, the breath coming hard and rasping in our chests.

It was after we'd begun to breathe a little easier that Faleecy John squeezed my arm and motioned with his head toward the tree. A little gray squirrel was venturing out on the limb that was hanging over us. He'd peer all about cautiously and then run a few steps. Then he'd stop and peer again and sit up and work his jaws. When he got right over us we laid as still as mice and he peered and stopped again. By then I reckon he had confidence in us, for when he stopped he commenced to jabber and scold for all he was worth. He'd chatter and bark and scold and then he'd stop and nibble at his paws. Then he'd start jabbering again.

And then we saw why he was taking on so. Over in the next tree started up another chattering and scolding, and the mate to the dark, furry little fellow in our tree came out to the end of a limb and jawed furiously at him. Back and forth the scolding went. She fussed and fumed at him, maybe for not bringing home enough to eat, and he fussed and fumed right back at her. His bark was a little gruffer, but hers was more constant. Every time he barked she barked a little faster. Faleecy John and I laid there and listened, and the longer we listened the funnier it got. "Jist like Ma an' Pa," Faleecy John whispered finally, and that was too much for me! I busted out laughing and the squirrels, startled and scared, ran away.

We got up then and brushed ourselves off, and still laughing went on down the road. I looked at my shirt, all dirty and torn, and felt of my face, bloody and mashed, and I knew I was a sight to behold. "I don't know what I'll tell Lucibel," I said.

"Jist tell her what happened," Faleecy John said. "She'd ort to know a man's got to take keer of hisself. An' if she don't know, hit's time she was learnin'."

Brave, bold words! But Faleecy John didn't have to face Lucibel!

Still and all, she took it right well. She sort of sniffed when she was washing my face and said she thought Faleecy John was taking a right smart on himself. Papa sucked on his pipe and forgot he hadn't lit it yet. "Did you knock him down?" he wanted to know.

"Yes sir," I said, "I reckon I did. Or he might just have got too tired to stand up any longer."

Papa struck a match and lit his pipe and then he laughed a little. "E'er time a Harbin can't lick a Squires," he said, "even giving him two years difference in age and weight, I want to know about it."

I had my doubts about that and I shook my head. "I don't know, sir," I said, "Faleecy John's a sunava-bitch when he's mad!"

Papa laughed until the pans rattled on their hooks behind the cook stove. He rocked in his chair and pounded his knees with his fists. He threw his head back and fairly roared. But Lucibel turned as red as a turkey cock's wattles, and she scrubbed my mouth out with hard-water soap.

What made it so bad was she had blackberry dumplings for supper and I couldn't taste a thing but the lye in that soap.

# six

I'VE ALWAYS thought it an odd circumstance that the first time I used this new skill Faleecy John had taught me was against Faleecy John himself.

School had been going on about a month, I reckon, and all the newness had worn off for me, and it was like I had always been going. The pattern was familiar and I had settled into it and was comfortable and easy in it. When I thought of my fear that first day, which I seldom did, it was to wonder what I had been afraid of. I have often taken notice that mostly we are afraid of the newness of a thing, rather than the thing itself. We like safe, familiar things, boy or man, and we venture into something new timidly and fearfully. An old fellow I used to know, lived over toward Lo and Be-

hold, told me once that he didn't rightly know whether
he loved his woman or not, but he shore as hell would
hate to do without her. Said he'd mortally hate to have to
change his way of doing. I reckon it's the same things
every day that make life certain and sure. Like the peg
behind the door where you hang your hat. Or the
corner by the chimney where you stand your gun. Like
the little cupboard under the stairs where you put your
boots. And like one woman's ways of redding up the
house. Once after me and Ida had been married a
couple of years we went to spend the day with some
folks we knew, and I remember it troubled me a heap
the way the woman had spread up her bed. Careless
like. I was used to Ida's neat tucking in of the coverlid.
It was the first time, I reckon, I stopped to think about
it. What was, was I'd just got used to Ida's ways.

Well, when school had been keeping about a month
I was liking it a heap. I was doing good in my books,
having run through the first reader in a flash. Rafe had
started me on an extra book and he heard me say my
lessons all to myself. I felt real proud of that. But over
and above the proudness was the pure liking for books
and reading. And I liked the new friends that I made.
Being an only child and, I reckon, a little lonely it was
like a miracle to me to be part of a noisy, milling gang
of twenty or thirty children. I went wild at recess time,
and often came inside when the bell rang, flushed and
hot with excitement, my heart beating so hard it took
me half an hour to breathe easily.

But far and away the best thing about school was
being with Faleecy John every day. He came by for me
each morning and waited at the gate if I wasn't already
there before him. And every evening we walked back
up the holler together. I could even reconcile myself

to not seeing him the Saturdays he had to help his pa, and the Sundays Papa and Lucibel took me with them to spend the day somewhere, because there was always Monday morning coming, and the whole long school week ahead. And I was guaranteed seven months of it. I had hated the school term bitterly before, because I had to stay behind. But I loved every minute of it, now. And I pushed February far down the calendar in my mind. To me, life was very wonderful those days.

Usually we went home the regular path up the holler, then followed the ridge road which led past our house and on out to the spur where Faleecy John lived. But sometimes we cut through the woods, or fields, just to go a different way. Where the woods were thickest we'd make out like we were Indians and we'd cut us sticks for tomahawks and hide behind the trees and split the air with bloodcurdling war whoops. Or maybe we'd fight the battle of Shiloh over again, from having heard Papa tell it the way Grandpa had told him. We'd sometimes hit a snag there, on account of neither one of us wanting to be Yankees. Most times we'd end up both being Rebels on a scouting expedition.

But one of our favorite games was to play like we was the Jesse James gang hiding out after robbing the bank. There was still a right smart talk in our parts about it. Some said it was Jesse himself, and others said it was Frank led the party. But whichever one it was, they robbbed the bank in at the county seat and killed one of the bankers. We liked that game a heap.

One afternoon we'd cut through the woods and had just come out at the fence to the lower pasture on our place. We climbed up on the fence and were playing like cowboys when we saw Papa and Silas Clark leading a cow across the pasture. Silas Clark was Papa's renter

and lived in the little house on yon side the lower
pasture.

Faleecy John and I pulled our rail-fence horses up
and sat them while we looked at the two men. "Cattle
rustlers!" Faleecy John whispered, and I nodded my
head. "Let's git 'em," he said, and he cut his horse
with his quirt and dug his spurs in.

"Yippee!" we yelled, "yippee!" and in a minute we
had them corralled. Then we slipped off our horses
and commenced closing in on them in the tall grass.
We snaked right up behind them before Papa saw us.

"Put 'em up," I yelled at him, "we've got you this
time!"

He grinned and raised his hands. "Well, I reckon
you fellers are too smart for me," he said, "I must be
slipping. Caught me dead-handed."

"Don't try to talk yerself outta this one," Faleecy
John warned him, "this is the last time you're goin' to
steal one of our cows! This time we're goin' to string
you up!"

"Now, boys," Papa said, "just give me one more
chance!"

But Faleecy John shook his head. "Nope. You've
done had yore chancet. We're goin' to hang you
higher'n a possum!"

Silas was standing there, not knowing what to make
of such foolishness, and I reckon it was taking note of
him made Papa stop playing, for he put his hands down
and a little frown came over his face. "Well, we'll have
to have the hanging another time, boys," he said. "I've
not got time today. And now you all go on home."

The game over, I wondered about the cow. "You
bought another cow, Papa?" I asked.

"No," he said. "Go on home now. Lucibel's looking

for you." And he and Silas Clark started walking on
across the pasture.

Faleecy John and I stood there a minute. It was
true that Lucibel always looked for us in the evening,
but then she didn't ever worry if we were a little late.
She knew two boys took their time getting home. She
hadn't ever scolded, not even the time when we didn't
get home until sundown, on account of building a dam
across the branch down in the holler. It just went like
an excuse to us.

Faleecy John kept watching the two men, his eyes
squinted in the sun, and suddenly he laughed. "Bet I
know what they're goin' to do."

"What?"

"C'mon an' I'll show you."

He angled off into the edge of the woods where they
couldn't see us and led the way around the north end
of the pasture over toward the back pasture. That was
where Papa kept the bull and he'd forbid me ever going
over there. He said the bull was mean and might
trample me. I felt skittery all at once and lagged behind. "Papa said for us not to go to the back pasture,
Faleecy John," I reminded him.

"You wanta see what they're goin' to do, don't you?"

Well, I did. I had a great surging feeling of excitement over the whole thing. Disobeying Papa, when
he'd said go on home. Going to the back pasture when
he'd said I was never to go there. It was like I was
charged with electricity all at once, tingling and prick-
ling, and feeling danger in the air. Wanting to go and
wanting to stay back. But wanting to go most. So when
Faleecy John went on, I followed.

We came up to the fence, which was the only wire
fence on the place on account of the bull being so

strong, and we sort of hid in a clump of bushes. But we could see everything that was going on. Growing up on a farm a kid learns pretty early about reproduction, and I knew in a general way how calves and colts were born. I knew that cows were taken to the bull, and that mares were taken to the stud, but I hadn't ever thought on what happened. Even as I watched it didn't dawn on me. I thought that old bull was pretty silly, snorting and tromping around, pawing the ground and raising a dust. And I had ragweed down my shirt and the bushes were hot and I was beginning to sweat and the ragweed was making me itch. I tugged at Faleecy John's sleeve. "Come on," I said, "let's go. I want a drink."

"Wait," he whispered, "ain't nothin' happened yit!" The sweat was shining on his face, standing in beads around his mouth and lips, and his eyes were bright and shiny. "Look at him," he exulted, his voice husky and whispery, "jist look at him! Ain't he wonderful? Ain't he powerful? Ain't he havin' hisself a time!" And his hands gripped the fence so tight his knuckles showed white. I was fascinated by the taut look on his face, the bright excitement in his eyes, the shiny, beady wash of sweat on his face, and I knew he had forgotten me in some strange, sweeping feeling that had gripped him and swept him beyond known barriers for me.

I looked across the pasture, then, and something of the same excitement gripped me, for the bull made his leap, and even I could tell that here was something primal, something strong and ruthless and impelling; something brutal, driving and instinctive. Something bewildering and confusing and frightening. Something of the root and source and stuff of life.

Faleecy John gripped the fence and his face was

white and tight. "Goddlemighty," he breathed, "look at him!"

I twitched at his sleeve again. "What's he doin?" I asked.

And Faleecy John told me. In small, simple, one-syllable words he told me. The words I'd seen scrawled in the outhouse at school. The words I'd heard older boys snickering over. The words that have their origin in the barn lot. They'd never meant a thing to me before. But now I knew. "That's the way ever'thing gits borned," Faleecy John finished. "Even babies."

"People . . . " I commenced to say, but my mind stopped before that implication.

"Why, shore," he said, "men are like that old bull, an' wimmin are like the cow."

Disbelieving I looked down the front of my overhalls, and suddenly, remembering my own small person, I knew he was saying true. But this thing in the pasture, now. That.

"How do you know?" I asked.

He laughed. "Ma and Pa. Times they don't wait 'til the fire goes down."

"Your own ma and pa?"

"Shore, silly! An' yore'n, too. Yer Papa an' Lucibel."

"No!" I said, "No! Not Lucibel!"

"How else you think you got made? You was their baby, wasn't you? Think they found you in a skunk cabbage?"

But a blind rage had taken hold of me and a sickening despair at this smearing of Lucibel. Everybody else, maybe. But not Lucibel. Never Lucibel! And I hammered at him suddenly with both fists, driving him into the bushes and hard against the fence. I was so mad I crawled all over him and rode him to the ground. He slipped down beneath me and I straddled him, just like he had the Combs boy, and in a crazy fury I pounded away at his face and head. "Take it back," I kept saying, "take it back!" and all the time the tears were running down my face and there was a salty taste in my mouth where I'd bitten my own tongue. Faleecy John heaved himself over and buried his head in his arms, not trying to fight back, and as the fury spent itself the power in my arms was drained away. And I knew it was hopeless.

I have known few moments in my life blacker than the one I knew then. I dragged myself up off Faleecy John and swiped the wetness off my face. I didn't even want to cry any more. If life could thus betray me, there was no use crying. There was no use anything. If Lucibel, who was all of beauty and joy and gladness to me, if Lucibel could be part of this ugliness, there was no use of anything.

Faleecy John turned over and sat up. He drew his knees up and laced his arms about them and looked at me. He didn't say anything for a minute, but when he spoke his voice was soft and kind. "Jeffie," he said, "it's all right when a man an' woman's married."

I shook my head.

"Yes it is," he said, and he reached out and pulled a string of grass and rubbed it through his fingers slowly. "Folks git married, an' then they's babies. An' babies are nice, Jeffie. As nice as little calves an' colts. They're all soft an' sweet-smelly, an' when you hold 'em they're round an' snuggly, an' they go all loose in yer arms. They's nothin' nicer than babies, Jeffie. I helt one oncet. Hit was Junie Tuckers's. An' how else would they be babies, if folks didn't git married an' make 'em?"

Stubbornly I shook my head.

"Hit's the way God made things, Jeffie," he insisted, "hit's bound to be all right if it was intended so." His voice went on talking, talking, and little by little the stubborn wall of ugliness inside of me began to crumble. The blackness and the despair ebbed away, and the tight knot in my stomach raveled out. Ah, Faleecy John! With a few short, brutal words he had torn my world down and stripped it of its beauty. And then reasonably, softly, gently, he built it back up for me. Almost, that is.

"Faleecy John," I said, "can I go home with you and take the night?"

It was all right. Faleecy John had made it all right. But I just didn't want to be with Papa and Lucibel that night. If I could be with Faleecy John he could keep it all right for me and maybe by tomorrow I could put it down inside me and look at Papa and Lucibel again. I didn't know if I could, but I knew I had to try.

"Why, shore," he said, "be glad to have you."

That was the first time I ever spent the night with Faleecy John. We had a heap of fun. Lydie made hoe-cakes for supper and I watched her pat them out with her hands, leaving the marks of her fingers. She baked them on a long, flat piece of tin that she propped up in the hot coals. When they were done, she rolled some little new yams out of the ashes to cool, and fried some side meat crisp and brown. She sent Faleecy John to the spring for the buttermilk and it was thick and buttery and cold . . . so cold it made your teeth ache.

Everything tasted better to me than what we had at home, and I ate so much I had to unbutton the sides of my overhalls. Lydie laughed and said she always liked to see folks have a good appetite. There sure was nothing wrong with mine that night!

After supper, when it was beginning to get dusky dark and the first whippoorwills were starting in to call, I had a funny feeling creep up in me. A sad, lost, whimpering sort of feeling. Hackberry Spur was so far from home, and the pines came up all around and darkened the sky, and the cabin was so lonesome way off to itself. Everything was strange and different, and there was nothing I could hold to. I felt strange even to myself. I didn't belong here. Jeff Harbin had no business here. My own identity fled, and it was like Jeff Harbin had gone away.

All at once I wanted to go home. I wanted the lamps lighted in the kitchen, and the heat from the big black stove in the corner, and the blue dishes on the supper table. But most of all I wanted Lucibel moving swiftly from the stove to the table, humming a little under her breath, and Papa sitting by the stove, maybe mending a piece of harness, and looking up every now and then to say something to Lucibel. I wanted to get myself back again. Get back into being Jeff Harbin. Back where I belonged.

I wanted desperately to go home, but I was ashamed to say so, for I had been the one to ask if I could come. I thought it was going to be a long night, and there was nothing to do but stay it out. But after the night work was done up Ben got out his banjo and tuned it up and started playing. He played a lot of jingly tunes I hadn't heard before, and he sang some of them. One of them fair set your feet to tapping. Faleecy John knew the words and he commenced singing, and directly I'd learned most of them, too.

> *Oh, Susanna, don't you cry fer me,*
> *Fer I'm goin' to Louisiana*
> *With my banjo on my knee!*

That was the way it went. And there was another one, he said was named the "Arkansas Traveler," and it had a lot of verses. Ben said he'd really ought to have a fiddle for it, but the banjo went right good I thought.

When the night had closed in Lydie spread down the pallet for me and Faleecy John and we went to bed. Not until after we'd gone outside and I'd got dew-damp in my hair. When the fire had died down we could see the stars through the holes in the roof, and that was when Faleecy John said he'd brushed the stars down in my hair.

I felt good lying there by Faleecy John, and I wasn't a bit sorry then I'd come. The room was dim and it had a friendly feeling with just the fire-glow shining on the walls. And Faleecy John's foot kept rubbing, soft-like, against mine. I turned over, and then I thought of something. I raised my head to see. I nudged Faleecy John. "Your pa hangs his overhalls on the foot of the bed, don't he?"

Faleecy John was sleepy and his voice was slow and quiet. "Why, shore," he said, "why?"

I giggled. "I thought he hung them in the wood shed!"

# seven

THOSE WERE good years. Fast-flying years, when I look back on them. But time is never fast for a youngun. The earth turns slow when you're seven or nine or eleven. A new sun comes up every day and rolls the slow hours across the sky, and from moon change to moon change feels like forever and enduring.

Spring starts easy-like, with the swell of buds in the thickets, the fan of a bluebird's wing spread to the sun, the sigh of the south wind through the winter grass. And then it swiftens and burgeons, greening the hills and the pastures, darkening the earth, and touching the dogwood with a clear, white flame.

One slow day spring gives itself to summer and the skies are a hot, bright blue, and the earth crumbles to dust and blows itself into spirals before a cranky, cross-tongued wind. Days are long, and nights are short, and along in August the stars fall like showers of golden rain. Sometimes, too, in August, the northern lights curtain the horizon with gauze, all green, shot with pink and lavendar, soft against the night.

Then summer lazes itself away, and fall brisks up the trees, pinches the late flowers and leaves them bruised, swirls a gusty wind through the haymows and corn shocks, tipping their skirts and leaving them bedraggled and unkempt.

Finally it laces the earth in hard and tight under a layer of ice and gives it over to winter. Then the north wind howls down the holler and screams around the chimneys, and the stars pull far back in the sky to give it room. The moon freezes hard as silver and rides bleak and high, lonesome as a ghost haunting a lonesome land.

These are the seasons of the year, but they ran together for Faleecy John and me until we never knew the start or the finish of any of them. Time to us was no longer than the day, or at most next week, or next month. Spendthrifts of time we were, using it, or throwing it away, and never counting any of it lost.

That first night I stayed with Faleecy John was the first of many nights we spent together, either at his house or mine. As regular as come Friday, we took the night together, and barring something uncommonly wrong, we never missed a turn. I went to his house one week, and he come to mine the next.

I got used to the cabin on Hackberry Spur. Got used to the chinking crumbling out from between the logs, and the floor boards sagging and rotting away and the make-do house plunder set around the room. I got used to the hogs rooting around under the house, and the dogs fighting them away. Got used to the dishwater-soaked back yard, and the chicken-scratched front yard. I even got used to the pines hovering the cabin under, and while their somber darkness made me uneasy, times, I never was again what you'd call homesick.

I got used to it all and it seemed to me we had the best times when I'd go to Faleecy John's. At least until Ben took to acting different, it seemed so. Lydie, knowing I loved her hoecakes so good, would always bake them when I was coming, and while she didn't have much to do with, she tried to make a little company supper on those Friday nights. She had a bleached feed sack she'd run some red stitching around, and she'd put that on the table for a cover. She'd one good plate wasn't chipped or cracked. She'd got it with Arbuckle coffee labels, and aimed to get the whole set but never got around to it. She'd set that plate for me. And once when I brought her some roses from Lucibel's bushes she bunched them in a little blue pitcher and put them in the middle of the table. "Did yer ma send these?" she asked.

"No," I said, "I just thought you'd like them."

Her mouth twisted funny, then, and I thought she was going to cry. But she just crimped her mouth straight and said, "You're a heap like yer pa." Then she set about dishing up supper, and she was extra nice and gay-like all evening.

Summers, after supper me and Faleecy John would go down to the branch in the holler and strip off and take a bath. The water wasn't over waist-deep anywhere, but that was enough to wash the sweat away and cool us off and leave us feeling clean and smooth. We'd splash each other and duck ourselves and dog-paddle around. We'd try seeing who could stay under the longest, and we'd clap rocks together under water to hear the queer, faraway sound.

Once when Faleecy John had his head under water I said something to him and he didn't answer when he came up. "Reckon you cain't hear under water?" he said when I told him. "I'll try again and you say something."

But he looked so funny with his head down and his backside up that I got tickled and fell over backwards and might nigh strangled to death before I could get my breath back. And Faleecy John might nigh drowned waiting for me to say something.

Winters, mostly we'd sit by the fire and roast chestnuts and pop corn. And Ben'd get out his old banjo and pick us a tune or two. He showed both of us how to chord it, and Faleecy John caught on right straight. But my fingers were all thumbs and the sounds that come out of that banjo when I got hold of it made about as much music as a tomcat yowling.

I reckon that was the way Faleecy John got his start picking a stringed instrument. Later he switched to a guitar. Said it was softer and sweeter. But he could take anything with strings, guitar, banjo, mandolin or fiddle, and make it sing.

On moony nights, sometimes, Ben'd run the hounds across the ridge after a possum or a coon. Faleecy John loved those times. There was something about the stilly night, and the belling of the hounds, and the frost-rimmed fields, and the trees stark against the moon, that excited and quickened him, and made him tireless. Partly it was the thrill of the chase, for there is nothing like the thrill of hunting once you have known it. But mostly it was because certain atmospheric qualities of beauty, certain attenuated textures of feeling, certain far-flung widenesses of emotion charged him with a vibrancy that set him flaming. He couldn't bear to look upon too much beauty, too much feeling, too much living. For he couldn't hold it all, and he couldn't stand not holding it.

Once, coon-hunting years later, we came out of the woods on a high, far meadow overlooking the valley of Little Lost Creek. The moon was late-riding, pale and misty, and the valley lay enchanted far below, the creek a silver ribbon wound among the trees. Out of the stillness an owl hooted . . . twice, mournful and forlorn. When I looked at Faleecy John his head was flung tall against the sky, and his arms hung straight down by his sides, fisted against his flanks. He was as tight as a fiddle string, and he never said a word. But the tears were rolling down his face and he left them roll, like he never even knew they were there.

When he came to my house it was fun, too. There was the pond down in the pasture and the raft we'd built. There were the apples and peaches and pears in the orchard to climb up and get. There were the colts and the calves and Lucibel's little fuzzy ducks in the barnyard. There was the hayloft in the big barn, and the watermelon patch over the hill. There were the big, wide, airy rooms, and the pretty blue dishes on the supper table, and the vittles always so plentiful.

And there were the horses. Papa let us ride the horses sometimes. He'd put the bridles on and lead them out to the upper pasture, and we'd crawl on from the fence rail, and go sailing around the pasture bareback. Faleecy John always liked to ride a little bay mare we had. And Papa usually humored him. She had a white star in the middle of her forehead, and that was her name . . . Star. Faleecy John always brought her something special to eat. An apple or a lump of brown sugar or something, and seemed like she knew him and waited for him. It like to killed him when Papa sold her.

We'd just got home from school and went straight out to the barn to see if we could ride. Papa said yes, and he allowed we were big enough to catch our own horses. We got the bridles and went out to the lot. There were four or five in the lot that afternoon, but Star wasn't there. We didn't take much notice of it, thinking Papa'd turned her in the pasture maybe, and Faleecy John caught him up a chestnut colt. We had our ride and didn't come in until almost dark. Lucibel was a little put out with us and hurried us. She said we had to eat right straight on account of Papa had to go to the county seat that night.

We washed up and sat down to the table, and Papa came in all dressed up in his town clothes, his hair slicked down, and his face shaved fresh. "You boys take good care of things tonight," he said, "I'll not get back until some time tomorrow. Get in plenty of cook wood for your mother, Jeffie. I've done up the rest of the work. And tomorrow you can start raking the leaves in the yard. I reckon most of 'em have fallen. But don't burn 'em until I get back."

I said yes sir to the cook wood, and no sir to burning the leaves. And added, "You got Star out in the pasture Papa? We didn't see her this evening, and Faleecy John rode the chestnut colt."

Papa shook his head. "I've sold her," he said, "she's not been foaling right the last two times, and I decided I'd better get rid of her and get as much out of her as I could."

"You've sold her!" Faleecy John said, and his face was as white as the tablecloth, and the fork he was holding clattered onto his plate.

Papa looked at him queer-like. "Why, yes," he said, "why?"

But Faleecy John just ducked his head and didn't say another word. Knowing how he had loved her I felt the sorriest for him. I tried to tell Papa. "Faleecy John nearly always rode Star," I said, "don't you remember?"

Papa looked at us both a minute and then he swallowed real hard. He folded his napkin and slipped it through the napkin ring. "I'm sorry, Faleecy John," he said finally, and his voice was real quiet. "I wouldn't have sold her if I'd thought."

Faleecy John flicked his head up quick and proud. "She was yore horse," he said, and it was like he had turned Papa's words back on him, just as quiet, but terribly proud. Like he wouldn't have anybody, even Papa, saying he was sorry to him. His mouth wasn't quite steady, but his words were.

Papa shoved his chair back and went around to kiss Lucibel good-bye. She patted his hand when he laid it on her shoulder, like she didn't mean him to worry too much about it and he smiled at her and went out the back door.

We dried the dishes for Lucibel and got in the cook wood, and then she said it would be a good night to have a little fire in the parlor and maybe play the organ. Usually that was a thing Faleecy John loved to do. The organ was bright and shiny with lots of fancy scrollwork over the front, and two little shelves at the top where Lucibel had set some vases. One had some feathers she had painted in it, and the other one had a bunch of dried grass she'd dipped in hot wax. I thought both were mighty pretty and I was awfully proud of the organ, too, since nobody else on the ridge had one.

Lucibel could play a few chords, and she'd pick out a song she knew in the hymn book, start pumping, and the organ would wheeze a minute or two, then it would make music. Me and Faleecy John would stand behind Lucibel, looking on the book to see the words, and sing with her. When we got started we'd likely sing all the songs we knew before we quit. Sometimes Papa would come in the parlor with us and help out, and then it was really good. But sometimes he had work to do and would be out around the place somewhere.

We played and sang a lot of songs that night, and I thought Faleecy John was feeling all right about the mare. He never named it again, and seemed like he loved the singing just as good as ever. And when Lucibel made us a big pot of hot milk with egg and nutmeg beat up in it and got out some cookies, he ate like always.

It was after we'd gone to bed it all came out. I had my own room, which is not common on the ridge for a boy on account most families being big and crowded for room. But our house was big and there was just me, so from the time I can remember I had my own place. Of course it was right next to Papa's and Lucibel's and the door opened into theirs. But still it was mine.

Lucibel had come to the door to see if everything was all right and had gone back in her room and blown out the light, and we had snuggled under the covers. I asked Faleecy John if he wanted a pillow-fight and he said no. So we talked a while, I disremember about what, and then I got drowsy and quiet and was just about to drop off to sleep when I felt the bed quivering. It waked me wide awake and just a little scared. I lay still, waiting, and it quivered again, and then I heard

Faleecy John snub back a sob. It went like he was choking. I reached out my hand and touched him, "Faleecy John," I whispered.

He drew back. "Don't," he said, but his voice was trembly. And then like he couldn't hold it back any longer he started crying and his body shook with it and the sounds of it were harsh and tearing. The crying came out of his chest like it was pulled out, and like it hurt terribly as it came. He tried to stop. I could hear him trying, but he couldn't, and it just got worse.

"What is it, Faleecy John?" I said, "what is it?" But he wouldn't let me touch him, and he couldn't say what it was. I thought I'd better tell Lucibel and was just slipping out my side the bed when she lit the lamp in her room, and directly she came through the door. "Faleecy John," she said, setting the lamp down on the dresser and going to the bed, "Faleecy John boy," and she put her arms around him and pulled him up close to her. She didn't ask him what was the matter, just like she already knew. She just held him tight against her and smoothed his hair and sort of rocked back and forth with him.

He cried harder for a minute or two, and then he got quieter. Finally he was still, and I took a deep breath, glad it was better. Lucibel held him on for a while and then she said, "My bed's too big and wide for me to-night! You boys come get in with me. One on one side, the other on the other, and I'll be safe in the middle!" She laughed and we scrambled out and ran and jumped into hers and Papa's big, wide bed. It was still warm from where she'd lain.

We giggled, and Lucibel said, "Now, isn't this better?" And she told us a story. When it was over we settled down, all three of us, and went to sleep.

Along toward first light I waked up feeling chilly and huddly and not knowing hardly where I was. I turned over, and then I remembered when I saw Lucibel. I raised up on one elbow to see Faleecy John over on the other side. And I had to laugh at what I saw, for Faleecy John looked exactly like a little puppy curled up against Lucibel. Just his nose was sticking out of her long, yellow hair spread all over the pillow. He still had one arm thrown across her and his head was snuggled down on her shoulder. She had her face turned so that her mouth rested against his cheek. I started to wake them, but thought better of it. So I tugged some cover over my way and snuggled back down and went to sleep again.

# eight

L IKE I SAID, those were good years, and swift gone. It wasn't hardly any time until Faleecy John was going on thirteen, and it was about then Ben commenced acting queer.

He never had been much account. Always content just to make out, which we considered poor-white-trashy in our parts. Many a good man has got his start renting, mind, and it's not to be held against him. But nobody with any pride wants to keep on renting forever and a time like Ben did. Seemed like he didn't care as long as he had a roof over his head and a little some-thing to put in his stomach. Mainly he liked to do as he pleased. If he took a notion to go fishing he never let the tobacco needing working stand in his way.

Same way with hunting. Although I reckon a good bit of what they had to eat came from the end of his fishing pole and his gun.

He was always sort of good-natured, too, in a heedless kind of way. Nothing hardly ever riled him, and he'd sing and pick his banjo right through the worst of Lydie's nagging. He'd wink one eye and pat his foot and work a new line in his song when she was at her worst. Something about the old woman's jaws aflapping. I'm not saying Lydie's nagging wasn't enough to drive a man to drink, for she hardly ever spoke a word that wasn't complaining one way or the other. But neither am I saying Ben's triflingness wasn't enough to drive a woman crazy. She had near about everything on the place to do, if it was done. I don't see how they either one made out to put up with the other. But they did right well for a good, long time, and then seemed like Ben got to getting mean.

Papa said it was the moonshine Ben got over at Enos Higgins' still, down at the foot of Lo and Behold, made him so mean. He did take to drinking mighty heavy, and he got to acting sully and scowly. That was all, at first. Quit picking his banjo and singing of a night. Just sat and looked at the fire, broody-like. His appetite fell off, too, and he'd always been one that liked his vittles.

He wasn't to say mean for a long while, but eventually he took to drinking heavier and heavier and then he got to knocking Lydie and Faleecy John around. He hadn't ever done that, that anybody had heard of. Folks shook their heads and allowed it was the drink. No good ever come of such.

Faleecy John had got his share of hickory tea, I reckon, like all the kids raised here on the ridge. But he hadn't ever been mistreated none. But now he came to school more and more often with a funny, scared look on his face, and with his backside too sore for him to sit comfortable. Ben wasn't using a limb on him any more. He'd taken to a horsewhip. Not that Faleecy John said much about it. He never. But I could tell he was pretty miserable, and what was worse, he didn't know what to make of it.

I told Papa and Lucibel about it one night at supper, and Lucibel's mouth set thin and straight, like it always did when she was displeased about something. "Mark," she said, and her hand shook when she poured his coffee, "you ought to do something about that!"

Papa put cream and sugar in his coffee and took a sip. "I don't know what it would be," he said. "A man can't go interfering with another man and his family."

"Couldn't you tell him that folks here on the ridge won't stand for him mistreating his family?"

"We've not got any actual proof that he is, Lucibel. Just Faleecy John's word that he's had two or three harder whippings than common. And we don't know what he did to deserve them."

Lucibel twitched her shoulders. "I reckon you'll have to wait until he half kills the boy!"

Which he almost did two or three nights later.

It was my turn to go home with Faleecy John to take the night, and Lucibel almost didn't let me go. She thought about it for quite a time, and then she said all right, but she didn't like it much, with Ben acting the way he was.

"I'll see to Jeffie," Faleecy John said, and she smiled at him kind of queer.

"I know you will," she said. But she let me go.

Ben wasn't home yet when we got there, and with it

getting on toward night, me and Faleecy John turned in and did up the night work. Faleecy John was splitting out cook wood and the axe was dull, so he gave it a turn or two on the grindstone. I reckon he must of slanted it a little too much, or something. Anyways he nicked it. Just a little nick it was, over at one edge. Wouldn't ever hurt the cutting edge at all. But it scared Faleecy John anyhow. "Pa'll give me hell fer that," he said, but he went on doing up the night work just the same.

We'd finished and were eating supper when we heard Ben coming. He was yelling and bellowing at the dogs as he came down the trail, and you could tell he had a load on. He came weaving in at the door and drew up and stopped when he saw us sitting around the supper table. He eyed Faleecy John and me, and then he commenced snickering and laughing like he'd thought of something funny. He tried to point his finger, but he couldn't hold it steady enough. "I see we got Harbins fer supper," he said, and that tickled him so that he fell over on the bed and laid there rolling and tumbling and laughing fit to kill.

Lydie had got white as a ghost and her hands shook so she couldn't hardly hold her fork. "Don't pay no mind," she whispered, and I ducked my head. I didn't aim to. I didn't want anything to get started. But I thought Lucibel was right and I shouldn't come any more for a while.

Directly Ben rolled off the bed and stumbled over toward the door. "Got to do up the work," he muttered, "got to git the work done up."

"I've already done up the work, Pa," Faleecy John said.

But Ben never paid him any heed. "Got the work to

do up," he said, and he kicked the door open and fell out on the porch. We heard him pick himself up and go rambling off.

"Mebbe he'll sleep it off out in the barn tonight," Lydie said, and she set to scraping out the dishes and redding up.

Faleecy John and I sat down by the fire, and it made me shiver to think how different it was. Nobody said a word, and the quiet was so thick it felt smothery. I noticed how Faleecy John kept rubbing his hands together, and I reckoned he was thinking, like I was, that Ben'd likely find the nick in the axe, and hoping he wouldn't. Not tonight when he was drunk, leastways. He might not be so mean about it come tomorrow when he'd sobered up.

We saw a glimmer of light out the window and knew Ben had managed to get the lantern lit, and now we knew for sure he was going to split some wood and would see the axe. There wasn't much use hoping he'd miss that little nick. A woodsman can tell the minute he hefts his axe if there's the least thing wrong with it. And Ben was better than most in the woods.

We didn't have long to wait. He let out a beller you could hear to Lo and Behold and come storming into the house waving his axe around mighty careless-like. "Who nicked my axe" he said, "who done it? Sunava-bitch don't know how to edge a axe ain't got no business atryin' it! Who done it?" And his face was as black as a thundercloud.

"I done it," Lydie said, quick-like and trembly. "I had to cut me some cook wood . . . " and her voice trailed off and whispered itself out against the walls.

Faleecy John looked at her, and then he squared himself around toward Ben. "She never done it," he said,

"I done it. She wouldn't try to edge no axe. I never meant to, but I don't reckon you'd believe it. Hit was dull, an' I jist give it a couple turns on the stone. Must of slanted it a leetle."

"You goddammed little bastard," Ben roared at him, "I'll teach you to nick my axe fer me! You'll wish you'd never been borned by the time I git through with you!" And drunk as he was he grabbed Faleecy John by the hair and started dragging him outside.

Faleecy John was squirming, trying to get loose, not saying a word, just twisting and turning, his face set like grim death. Lydie run at Ben and took hold of his arm. "Not tonight, Ben," she begged, her words running together on account of her crying, "Please, Ben, don't. Ben, you'll kill him if you whup him tonight. You don't know what yer doin'!"

"That's what I aim to do," Ben said, and he dragged Faleecy John on out to the barn.

I stood there by Lydie, hearing her weeping and moaning, and I thought I'd rather die than listen to what was going to happen. Trying, too, to think of something I could do. My mind dodged around like a rat trying to get out of a trap, and I couldn't think of anything.

And then I heard the first lick, and Lydie's legs folded under her and she sagged down on the ground like she had fainted. They came mighty close together for a drunk man to be laying them on, I thought, and I thought maybe Ben did aim to kill him at that. Without knowing what I could do with it, I grabbed up a chunk of stovewood and commenced edging over towards the door. Lydie stirred a little, and then it came to me we might together get Ben stopped.

"Lydie," I said, "if you're not afraid to try it, maybe we can help Faleecy John."

She just moaned, but she was staggering up, and I knew she could hear me. "Listen, Lydie," I said, "you go in and try to get hold of Ben's arm and hold on as tight as you can. I'll sneak in back of him and hit him with this chunk of wood. The only thing is, he'll likely get in a lick or two at you before I can lay him out. But I don't know any other way to do it. We'll have to knock him out to get him stopped."

She didn't even answer me, just commenced running to the barn, and I followed right on her heels. The lantern light wasn't very bright, but it gave enough light for me to see enough to turn my stomach. Ben had Faleecy John stripped and tied to a wagon wheel, and he'd cut the blood every lick he'd given him. It was running down Faleecy John's back, and there was thin red stripes that lapped clean around his waist where the end of the whip had laced him. His head was leaning against the wheel, and for one everlasting moment I thought maybe he was already dead, his face was so white.

Lydie went flying in under Ben's arm when he had it raised for another lick, and she grabbed it with both hands and held on tight, swinging her whole weight on it, so that he had to bend under it. He cussed and flung around trying to get rid of her, but she held on. I gripped the chunk of wood with both hands, and when he swung around again I laid his scalp wide open with it. I never thought but what it would kill him, and I never cared. The sight of Faleecy John had turned me crazy, and when Ben went down I reckon I would have pounded his head to a pulp if Lydie hadn't grabbed my arm. "That's enough, Jeffie," she said, "that's enough. Come help me with Faleecy John."

He wasn't even unconscious, for all his face was so white. He'd just been leaning against the wheel to bear him up, and I give you my word there hadn't been a sound out of him. I reckon he would of died before he'd have cried out. We untied him and helped him in the house and Lydie washed his back and smoothed some kind of salve on it. He sort of grunted once, then, but that was all.

We went to bed, but Lydie went up to the barn to see about Ben. When she came back she said he'd be all right and she'd just left him to come to himself up at the barn. She went to bed, too, then, and was snoring before the fire died down. I reckon she was plumb worn out with everything.

I knew Faleecy John's back was hurting him, for he kept moving around easy-like, and he had to lay on his stomach and he never could sleep that way. Finally he sat up in bed and reached for his shirt. I sat up, too. "Sh-sh-sh," he hissed at me, "don't make no noise to wake Ma. I'm goin' to leave out. This very night, Jeffie. I don't aim to take no more of this. I don't know what's got into Pa, but I'm not aimin' to stay an' take no more. I'm goin' to run away."

My hands chilled and my teeth chattered. "Where you going?" I asked.

"I've not thought of that yit. But I will." He was prowling around in the dark and I slipped into my overhalls. "What you doing?" I said.

"Gittin' my other shirt an' overhalls. If you're dressed, you kin look in the cupboard there an' git some cornbread an' meat to take along, but don't make no noise."

Quiet as a mouse I sneaked over to the cupboard and slid a hunk of bread and several pieces of meat into my pockets, and then the door squeaked as Faleecy John eased it open. I slid down the wall after him and he latched the door behind me. We padded across the porch and the grass but it wasn't until we were well up the trail that we risked talking.

"We'll go down the road as far as yore place," Faleecy John said, then, "an' I'll go on from there by myself. But I got to git you home first."

"I'm going with you." I'd been thinking about it, and I knew that I wasn't going to be left behind. Wherever he went and whatever he did, I wanted to be there.

"Naw," he said, "I'd git along better by myself. An' anyways, Lucibel would weary herself to death."

I'd thought of that, too, and while it brought a sickness to my stomach I didn't see any way around it. Lucibel would know I had to go with Faleecy John, and while I knew in reason she would worry, I had a feeling she'd understand. It was Papa I didn't know about. But I had to risk that.

"I'm going," I said, "and there's nothing you can say will change it."

"Listen, Jeffie," Faleecy John said, "I'm might nigh thirteen an' in my last year at school. I've been thinkin' hit'd be a good idee if I was to go over to another one of the settlements an' hire out to work. I'm big enough to do a man's work, all but, an' hit won't be no trouble fer me once I git away. You know yore folks is not goin' to let you do a thing like that, even if you was big enough!"

I hadn't thought of his doing a thing like that. I reckon my thinking was more romantic, but I'd thought of us going off down the river, maybe on a raft we made ourselves, like Huck Finn. Too much reading, that was me. But when he spoke I knew he was right. And I knew I'd just be in his way. "Have you thought where to go?" I said.

He thought for a while before answering. "I'd thought some of headin' fer the Persimmon Ridge settlement. Sim Parker over there's kin to Ma, an' I reckon he'd take me in."

That made sense to me, too, and then I thought of another thing. "I'll go over there with you. I can get back before I'm even missed. They think I'm spending the night with you, and won't be looking for me back until late tomorrow evening. I can make it easy."

"Hit's a long walk over there an' back," he said, "think yore legs kin hold out?"

But I could tell from his voice he was glad I wanted to go. "I know they can," I said stoutly, although I knew what lay before them. It was six miles to Persimmon Ridge, unless you cut through the hollers. "You going by the road?"

"Naw, we'll take the hollers. Save a heap of time."

We trudged on, and when we passed our place it lay dark and remote from the road. I thought of Papa and Lucibel asleep there, unknowing of Faleecy John and me passing in the night, and I thought of my own bed in the room right next. For a minute I wished to be turning in at the gate. But I put it behind me and kept walking beside Faleecy John.

We didn't talk much. This was such a big step for Faleecy John to be taking, and it held so much for both of us that I reckon we both had it on our minds. We turned off down the second holler, which angled across Little Lost Creek bottoms and would bring us out on Sawtooth over toward Lo and Behold. Persimmon Ridge was a spur of Sawtooth, and we ought to hit it about half way down.

It was powerful dark going down through the holler, but it's always easier to find your way down than up,

and we came out at Little Lost Creek without any
trouble. We waded the creek and headed up toward
Sawtooth. It seemed to me we commenced climbing
too soon, but I was leaving the leading to Faleecy John
and never said anything. And where he mistook the
trail I don't know, but pretty soon we were going
through some mighty rough places. I didn't know
much about this country and I still thought Faleecy
John knew where he was, but it worried me some to be
clambering around over those rocky cliffs and ledges
in the deep of night.

We kept going, and I was beginning to get winded
and was wondering just how far my legs would take
me, when Faleecy John stopped. "Jeffie," he says,
"We're lost. I don't no more know where we're at than
nothin'."

I pulled up beside him and heaved to get my breath.
But I wasn't scared. Uneasy, maybe, but not scared. I
allowed Faleecy John would figure it out. "What'll we
do?" I says.

"Camp right where we're at, wherever that is. Wait
'til mornin'."

It was late October and the nights had a right sharp
chill in them. We both had on a coat. Those short
jacket things boys wore when I was a youngun. But
neither one of them had much weight to them, and that
was all the covering we had. We hadn't brought a
lantern, of course, and I figured we didn't have any
matches. I knew I didn't. But Faleecy John commenced rummaging around in his coat pockets and
come up with a handful. He said kind of sheepish-like
that he'd been starting to smoke some.

We piled up some leaves and set them to burning and
then dragged up some wood and built up a good fire.

It felt fine, too. By the light we could tell we were in a
blowdown, with tree laps all around us. It sure looked
a mess all right, and I couldn't see how we could have
got right in the middle of it without more trouble than
we'd had. It was going to be something to find our way
out of come morning, too. But morning was time
enough to worry about that.

We cleaned the ground all around the fire so it
wouldn't spread, and piled leaves up to one side to
make us a bed. Then we ate some of the cornbread and
meat and laid down. As far as I know we were asleep
by the time we'd got good settled. I, for one, was
whipped out.

It was broad daylight when we woke up the next
morning, and when we took a look around we knew we
had us a time on our hands. That blowdown was about
the worst I ever saw! If we'd been in the midst of a
jungle thicket we couldn't have been in any worse trap.
The trees were lapped so bad that in places there wasn't
anything to do but get down and crawl.

Faleecy John took his direction and we started out,
but if you've never tried traveling in deep woods in
strange country, you wouldn't know how lost and un-
certain you can feel. Even grown men get lost sometimes in the woods, and sometimes in woods they've
been in time and again. A familiar place can all at once
look queer and strange to you, and if you know it's a
strange place and all you've got to go on is your direc-
tions, you're likely to wind up going in circles.

And I reckon that's what we did, for we wandered
that whole day and never once got out of that blowdown. We kept going and going and going, until we
were both clawed and scratched by the briars and
brambles, our clothes torn, and our legs and feet sore

and aching, and we thought we were going straight. It felt like it. We kept thinking over the next rise would surely be the end of it. But over the next rise was just more blowdown.

Once we came to a branch, and we drank our fill and sat down beside it to eat the last of our bread and meat. If we'd only known it that branch would have led us back to Little Lost Creek, but it seemed to us like it was running in the opposite direction. We were that turned around. So we just crossed it and went on.

First dark was coming when we finally gave up, trembly and scared and sick at heart. And getting mighty hungry, too. We sat and leaned back against a down log. Faleecy John put his head down on his knees and I could see his legs trembling. Mine felt the same way. "Are you skeered, Jeffie?" he said.

"Yes," I said. There wasn't any use trying to pretend now.

"So'm I," he said, "but we got to think of what to do."

He was quiet a long time. "They'll be huntin' fer us by now," he said, finally, "yore folks, I mean. They'll know by now we're gone. Best thing fer us to do, as I see it, is to build up a big fire an' set right here by it 'til they come. They kin see the fire a long ways off, an' come up on us quicker thataway. We cain't git out of this blowdown by ourselves, an' the best thing is jist to let them find us."

Yes, that would be best. But I shivered when I thought of all the hills and all the hollers and all the deep, dark woods. Maybe they wouldn't come up on us in time. Maybe they wouldn't ever come up on us. Maybe we'd just stay here in this blowdown and starve to death and all they'd find when they did find us would be our bare, bleached bones. Fear rose up like an animal inside me and clutched me by the throat. I had a frantic feeling of wanting to start out again to find the end of this crazy overlapping of down trees. To scratch through them and crawl under them and come out in the clear. Where we could see the sun overhead and walk a trail again. It was out there. Somewhere. If we could just find it! But I knew Faleecy John was right, and we had best sit here and keep our fire going.

Like the night before we raked up the leaves and brought up limbs and branches and started our fire. And then we hugged against it, hovering it close, for a small, cold rain sieved through the trees to add to our misery. We fed the fire until it was a bright, leaping blaze, and then we raked the leaves up around us to try to keep out the damp and the cold. We huddled together, and I don't know whether it was the wet, or the cold, or the fear, or the tiredness, or all of them put together made me commence shaking, but it was like I had a chill and couldn't stop. My teeth chattered and my backbone shook until it felt like it was coming unjointed.

"You cold, Jeffie?" Faleecy John asked.

I couldn't answer. I just burrowed closer.

He reached out and pulled me up close to him and put his arm around me. Then he put his other arm around me and held me tight. My chill shook us both, but gradually the warmth from his body soaked through me and the chill eased off.

"I'll tell you a story, Jeffie," he said, then. "Listen. I'll tell you a story." And he started telling the story of Goldilocks and the Three Bears. Lucibel used to tell it to us when we were little. I remembered how she would put an arm around each one of us, and rock back and forth in her little low-backed rocker, and her voice would rise and fall with her rocking. " . . . there was the papa bear . . . and there was the mama bear . . . and there was the little baby bear!"

I laughed and stuck my cold nose under Faleecy John's ear. It was so funny, him telling a big boy like me about the little baby bear! He squeezed me. "You hush," he said, "you hush, Jeffie, and listen!" And his voice went on and on, just like Lucibel's, rocking and rocking. I went to sleep before the story was finished.

The next I knew Papa was shaking me awake, and I came up out of my sleep like it had all been a bad dream. But there was the fire, and Papa, with tears rolling down his face, asking me if I was all right . . . if I was hurt or sick . . . and thanking God they'd seen our fire! Silas Clark was with him and two or three other men. But not Ben. They were all standing around the fire, everybody talking at once. Their horses were tied in the bushes, and their faces were clawed and scratched almost as bad as ours. "Hit's a God's blessing you younguns thought to build up that fire," they said, "we'd never have found you else!"

"It was Faleecy John thought of it," I told Papa, "it was Faleecy John."

And then Faleecy John and I were trying to tell our story, leaving out some and going back to pick it up again, the way you'll do when you're excited and there's so much to tell. But Papa said that could wait until we got home, that what we needed now was food and bed. So they took us up on the horses with them and brought us home. Papa felt big and strong as I sat in front of him riding home, his arm around me and his chest there for me to lean on. I never had thought how big and strong he could be, and it came over me how good he was, too. He hadn't scolded a bit. And his arm around me hugged me tight and safe.

When we got home Granny was there, for Lucibel had gone almost crazy with worry and fear and Papa had sent for Granny to put her to bed. She got up though when we came in, and hugged and cried over both of us. But she was shaking and trembling like a leaf.

"Git on back to bed, Lucibel," Granny said finally, "I'll take keer of 'em."

I was about half asleep, but I know that Granny stripped us both and washed us, and when she saw Faleecy John's back she showed it to Papa. His face got black and thundery looking. When she had clean night-shirts on us she fed us soup and hot milk and then she tucked us into bed. When she pulled the covers up around us she stood for a minute looking down at us. Faleecy John was already beginning to snore.

The bed was so soft and I was so warm and safe I could barely see and hear her. I remember the pucker of snuff in her lip, and that she turned away to spit in the fire. And I remember that when she'd spit she said, "The boy looks a heap like you, Mark."

It sounded so far away, and her voice was so flat and dry that it floated wispy and thin through the haze of sleep. But it pleased me mightily. I'd always wanted to look like Papa. I pushed the edges of drowsiness back far enough to widen my eyes and smile at Granny. Only she wasn't smiling. Her face looked gray and tired and she was looking at Papa with a queer, funny look on her face. And Papa's face was gray and tired, too, and Papa was looking at Faleecy John like he hadn't ever seen him before.

I couldn't hold it back any longer, the tiredness and

the sleepiness. I closed my eyes and let the feather bed under me float me down and down and down. The echo of Papa's voice went down with me, like it was drowning in the softness and the feathery warmth of the bed. "God," it said, "God! God!" And I thought it was funny I could hear it three times.

I took the echo along with me and drifted off on a lazy, fleecy cloud of sleep, soft and dreamy and safe.

# nine

LUCIBEL let us sleep the next day, and I reckon it must have been the middle of the morning when we got up. She fixed us a big breakfast, with hot biscuits and ham and honey in the comb, and teased us about being sleepyheads. She was all smiles and happy, looking like a bright yellow flower, with her yellow hair, and dress sprigged all over with yellow. She flew around the kitchen, humming to herself like she did when she was feeling good, and the sun was lazy and warm through the kitchen door.

"No need to hurry," she told us as we ate. "Papa sent word last night they'd found you all, so Lydie wouldn't worry. And he said he'd take Faleecy John home this afternoon."

I wished he didn't have to go at all. I wished he could just stay and live with us. But of course I knew he couldn't. You have to stay with your own folks, and Faleecy John belonged with Lydie and Ben. But I couldn't help naming it just the same. "Wouldn't it be nice, Lucibel, if Faleecy John belonged to us, and could stay with us all the time?"

She laughed and the ripple of it went into all the corners of the room. "Now, wouldn't it?" she said, "wouldn't that be something?"

We hadn't heard Papa come in, and it startled me when he spoke. "Careless words can be the starting of discontent, Lucibel." His voice roughed the warm, lazy air like a growl of thunder, and Lucibel looked at him strangely. He flushed under her look and turned to us. "You boys through eating? I need someone to move the cows to the lower pasture. I've got the horses already saddled."

Like a flash we were out the door into the winey, hazy day. We could be real cowboys today, taking a herd across the long, dry trail of the west! We whooped and hollered out to the barn lot, Papa coming easy behind us. But we stopped short when we got to the barn. For there was a bay mare, for all the world like Star, saddled and waiting for Faleecy John. He turned and looked at Papa, and then without saying a word he went and rubbed his hand down the mare's flank. Papa didn't say anything either, and I got a choky feeling in my throat. For I knew in reason he'd gone this morning while we lay asleep and bought the mare. I hated that I had felt hard toward him for selling Star. And I hoped that if Faleecy John had felt as bad as I did, he felt as good as I did now.

It was a glad, fine day that we had, and then late in

the afternoon Papa and I took Faleecy John home. Lucibel came out to the buggy when we were ready to go. She put her hand on Papa's arm and looked up at him. "You'll talk to Ben, Mark?" she said, and Papa nodded. He gathered up the reins, but Lucibel was still standing there. "I'll declare, Mark, if you're not taking it worse now that it's over than you did before you found the boys," she said, and she gave his arm a little pat. "You're not coming down with something, to look so peaked and worn, are you?"

Papa smiled at her. "Just had time to think what might have happened, I reckon," he said.

Lucibel laughed and stepped back. "No use worrying about spilled milk. It's over and done with now," she said, "and no great harm."

Papa looked at her queer-like, and then he slapped the reins against the mare's back. "We'll not be gone overly long."

"Don't get into trouble, Mark," Lucibel warned, her finger plucking at her mouth in a way she had when she was troubled.

"I'll not," he promised, and he wheeled the buggy down the road.

Faleecy John was fearing going home, you could tell. You could tell by the quietness that sat on him, and by the tremble that shook over him from time to time. Papa looked down at him and saw his hands rubbing his knees and he laid his own big hand over Faleecy John's. "I doubt it'll happen again, boy," he said, "I'm aimin' to talk to your pa . . . " his hand jerked sudden-like, but he steadied it, "to Ben," he says.

"Yes sir," Faleecy John said, but it was like he didn't think it would do much good.

Papa sucked in his breath, and then he cut the mare

with the whip and she jumped so fast and quick it popped all our necks, nearly threw me over the wheel, and blew Papa's hat off in the road. Everybody laughed and I jumped out and ran back to get the hat. I reckon it made us all feel better to laugh a little.

Papa told us how it had been the day before. Lydie hadn't thought it amiss when she'd got up Saturday morning and found us gone. At first she thought maybe we were somewhere around the place, and when she'd cooked breakfast and we didn't come she just allowed we'd gone to my house. And didn't know but what it was best. She was afraid for Faleecy John when Ben roused up. And she was right glad he wasn't there.

Ben had slept through until eight or nine o'clock and then had come to the house groggy and sully, either not remembering anything that had happened the night before, or not naming it if he did. She'd fed him and he'd rolled back up in the covers and gone to sleep again.

It wasn't until Lucibel commenced to get uneasy over me not coming home and sent Papa over to get me that anybody suspicioned a thing. Papa said he knew in reason what had happened the minute Lydie told him about the whipping, and he said his heart had sunk clean to his toes, for there was an awful lot of woods and hollers for two little chaps to get lost in. He said if he'd of started out without reasoning about it, the state he was in right then, they might never have found us. But he made himself think where we would have headed. And knowing Lydie's kin lived over toward Persimmon Ridge he figured they'd better start looking in that direction. For he said it stood to reason Faleecy John would head for some place he'd be certain of welcome.

He'd got the men together and before dark they were on the way. They went the road first, and went clean to the settlement, hoping to find us there. But when nobody'd seen or heard of us they turned back and commenced to search along the way. It was Silas Clark remembered the old trail across by Little Lost Creek and allowed we might of taken it for a short cut, and that was how they happened to see our fire. The blow-down wasn't far off the trail, but it was so thick and so jung!y we might never have found our way out of it.

"It was a smart thing to do, Faleecy John," Papa said, "to build that fire and sit and wait for us. That was smart thinking. Not everybody would have thought of it. How'd you happen to have matches?"

Faleecy John cut a glance at me, like he thought I might have told. I shook my head behind Papa's back. And then Papa laughed. "How old are you Faleecy John?"

"Goin' on thirteen."

"Little young for smoking, aren't you?"

"But it was right handy I had them matches!" Faleecy John flared up.

Papa's face sobered. "It was that! It was that, Faleecy John."

And that's all was said about the smoking.

When we got to Faleecy John's, Lydie came out to meet us. She was never given much to showing her feelings, and she didn't make over Faleecy John the way Lucibel had done over both of us. You couldn't tell if she had wept any, and there was no sign of worry on her face. It looked like always . . . brown, thin, strained, and wrinkled around the eyes and mouth. She laid her hand on Faleecy John's shoulder when he jumped out of the buggy, and that was all. It was Papa she spoke to.

"I'm beholden to you, Mark," she said, and her voice was level and dry.

"Is Ben here?" Papa asked, wrapping the lines around the whip socket.

"He's up in the woods lot."

"I want to talk to him. But first there's a thing I want to ask you." And he got out and tied the mare to the fence.

Faleecy John and I sat down on the edge of the porch and Papa and Lydie walked away. They went clean over to the edge of the pine woods. We could see them, but we couldn't hear a thing. Not even when Lydie commenced to cry. We could see her lean up against a piney tree, and we could see her shoulders sagging down, and we saw her put her hands over her face. We saw Papa take her hands down and hold them a minute, and then turn them loose. And we saw him looking out across the fields, back toward our place, a long, long time. It seemed to me his shoulders had sagged down some, too. We saw him turn, then, and start talking to Lydie, and he talked for quite a spell. "Likely," I whispered to Faleecy John, "he's telling her to let him know if your pa gets out of hand again."

Faleecy John nodded. "Likely," he said.

But just then we heard a funny mewling sound under the porch, and we lost interest in Papa and Lydie. We crawled under the edge to see what it was, and Faleecy John let out a yell. "Dogged if the bitch hasn't whelped! Look here, Jeffie. Look at all these pups." And we started wiggling fast back toward them.

There were seven of them, as pretty little hound pups as you ever saw! Black and tan, like the bitch, with not so much as a scar of white to mar them. I wanted one. The worst way, I wanted one. We picked them up and fondled them and looked them over. There were five males in the litter, and I'd have been happy with any one of them, but one especially I kept coming back to. He had more tan on him than the others, and looked lighter because of it. I reckon my wish for him stuck out all over me. I'd put him down and then I'd pick him up again. I couldn't keep my hands off of him.

"You like that un?" Faleecy John said.

I couldn't trust my voice. I was afraid it would give me away. I just nodded and put the pup down careless-like.

"You kin have him soon as he's big enough."

The promise made my heart bulge up in my throat. "Will Ben let you give them away?"

"This here's my bitch, an' I'll give her pups to anybody I like, see! Pa's not got nothin' to say about it! I raised her from a pup, an' I'll do as I see fit about her pups!"

And that was the way old Snooper came to me. Best fox hound ever ran these hills, he was. And he ran them for eighteen years. Until he was blind and deaf and toothless. He was blind that afternoon, but it was from newness of age, not oldness. He looked more like a rat than anything else. But he was beautiful to me. "When will he be big enough?" I asked, running the soft satin of his ears through my fingers.

"Six weeks," Faleecy John answered. "We'd best leave 'em be, now. I'll watch him fer you, an' bring him when he's big enough."

When we crawled back out from under the porch I went tearing off to tell Papa, but he was gone and Lydie was standing in the edge of the piney woods alone. She looked at me when I ran up, out of breath and pleased to pieces, and she smiled although her eyes were still wet.

"Where's Papa," I wanted to know.

"He's gone to talk to Ben," she said, and she ran her hand across my hair. I didn't like it. Her hand was so rough and calloused it caught in the hair and pulled. I wanted to draw back, but I was afraid of hurting her feelings. "Jeff Harbin," she said, and her voice was low and soft-like. "Jeff Harbin." And she suddenly drew her hand away and grabbed her apron to her eyes and ran away toward the house. I stood puzzled and watched her go.

When Papa came back from the woods lot he walked fast and stiff, like a man holding tight to himself. He got in the buggy quick, and when I came running all he said was "Get in." Then he whipped up the mare and wheeled the buggy around into the ruts of the road and we went off up the hill at a fast trot. I wanted to tell him about the puppy, but there was a frown on his face so dark I was afraid to open my mouth. So neither of us said a word all the way home.

He let me out by the back door and drove on to stable the horse. I went scampering into the house. Lucibel was dishing up supper. Breathlessly I told her about the puppy. "Faleecy John's dog has got pups," I said, "seven of them! And he's going to give me one. Just as soon as it's big enough he said I could have it."

"Now isn't that nice?" she said, stopping by the stove to turn and look at me. Her face was flushed from the heat of the stove and her hair was in little curls across her neck. Suddenly I loved her more than anything in the world and I flew across the room to fling my arms around her. She was so yellow and blue and clean and sweet, and she was Lucibel, and there wasn't anyone else so beautiful or so good. I was so glad she wasn't Lydie!

She hugged me tight for a minute then loosened my

arms. "Your papa will be in in a minute and I must get supper on the table."

"But isn't it fine about my dog?"

"Fine!" she agreed, "just fine!"

When Papa came in her eyes flew to his face, but he shook his head. She went to him and held up her face to be kissed. "Did you hear about Jeffie's dog?" she said.

"Dog?" Papa looked at me. "You didn't tell me about any dog, son."

"No sir," I stammered, "I didn't want to bother you."

He sat down and drew me between his knees. "I'm sorry if I looked bothered, Jeffie. Now, what's this about a dog?"

I told him, then, bubbling over with it, explaining what a beautiful dog it was, describing its color, measuring its length and size, giving him all the details, and he listened soberly. When I had finished he agreed that it sounded like a mighty fine dog, and he was mighty proud Faleecy John had given it to me. He said he could hardly wait, himself, for the six weeks to pass so we could bring him home. I sighed contentedly. Papa and Lucibel were so satisfying. It was so good that I belonged to them, and not, for instance, to Ben and Lydie. I felt a deep pity for Faleecy John, and I thought how unfair it was that you couldn't have anything to say about who your own folks were to be. You came to them, without your want or wish, and then either it turned out good, like it had for me, or bad, like it had for Faleecy John. The mystery of it was beyond my thinking, and I gave it over, but not yielding my thought that it was still unfair.

I was almost asleep that night when Papa and Lucibel started talking. Their room was dark and I knew they'd gone to bed, and like so many times, they were talking before going to sleep. The sound of their voices in the dark had been a comfort to me more than once. It went something like the purling of Little Lost Creek around the white rocks in the stream bed. Rise and fall and murmur, low and soft. But tonight I could hear the words and I couldn't help but listen.

"What happened, Mark?"

"Nothing much. I told him about Silas buying his own place and that I was going to need another renter, and offered him the place. He said he'd rather starve to death than be beholding to a Harbin."

"But why? He's always rented. Looks like he'd rather have that good little house and work for you than to keep on over on the spur where they can't hardly keep body and soul together!"

"One man can't ever figure another's reasons, Lucibel. Ben's pretty come-easy, go-easy, and maybe he don't want to move. Over there he can do about as he pleases. Work when he gets ready. Leave it go when he wants. Maybe he don't want to work like he knows he'd have to, working for me."

"He's just no-good, shiftless trash, that's what. Lydie'll keep on 'til she drops dead in her tracks, and Faleecy John'll have to carry the biggest part of the burden in another year or so. That's what I hate so bad about it. It's not right for that boy to be raised up the way he is."

There was a stillness for a time. Then Lucibel went on. "Did you tell Ben folks around here weren't going to stand for him whipping the boy like that any more?"

"Yes."

"What did he say?"

"Told me to mind my own business. Like I expected him to."

I heard the bedsprings squeak and I knew Lucibel

had flounced angrily. "Well, I never! I reckon he's to be allowed to kill the boy and we're all just to stand by and see it done. I hope you told him different!"

"I told him if the boy was whipped again with a horsewhip, I'd horsewhip *him* myself."

"I reckon that fixed him!"

"I don't know. He just sulled and didn't say any more. I left then."

There was a big sigh, and quiet, and then Lucibel's voice was warm and sweet. "You're a good man, Mark Harbin! You know how much I love you?"

I laughed in the dark. All my life I'd seen them play that game. Lucibel would say, "You know how much I love you?"

And Papa would laugh and ask, "How much?"

And Lucibel would hug him tight and say, "Up to the sky!" And Papa would always hold her close and bury his nose in her hair, like he was smelling of a sweet, yellow flower.

Tonight I didn't hear it all, for Papa tiptoed across the room and directly the door between squeaked on its hinges as he eased it to. But I didn't have to hear it, for I knew what he was going to say.

# ten

**B**EN CHANGED his mind about renting from Papa, but he didn't say why. Lucibel reckoned it was Lydie needled him into changing. But Papa never hazarded a guess. It made no difference to me, I was so tickled that Faleecy John would be living close by. I knew in reason after what had happened that Papa and Lucibel were going to cut down on me going over to Hackberry Spur, and I was hating the thought of it. And, too, I didn't know but what Ben'd make Faleecy John quit coming to our house. So I nearly went wild with joy when Papa came home one evening and said Ben had changed his mind. Papa didn't look any too glad himself. I reckon he knew he'd be in for it, trying to get any work out of Ben. But Lucibel and I were so tickled for Faleecy John that we more than made up for it.

Now, you can rent two or three ways on the ridge. One is to rent a house and piece of land outright. It's like you owned it then, as far as doing what you will is concerned. You can crop it the way you please, and you're your own boss as far as working it goes. An up-and-coming man had usually rather rent that way than any other, and he'll tend the land like it was his own, making it pay and keeping it built up. He'll take care of the house and property and turn it back to you as good as the day he rented. But Papa wouldn't never rent that way. Said there was too much chance of getting a shiftless, do-less sort of man who'd ruin the land and property.

Another way you can rent is on a share-crop basis. That's just what it sounds like. The farmer furnishes a house and garden patch, the land and fertilizer, seed and equipment, to make the crops, and the tenant furnishes the labor. The tenant gets a third or half of the crop . . . whatever figure is agreed on between him and the farmer. Papa never would rent that way, either. He liked to work his own crops.

The way Papa rented was more like hiring help. He furnished a good, tight little house with a fenced yard and garden patch, and good henhouse and barn. And then he paid his renter by the month to work for him . . . at whatever jobs he had in mind. I reckon he never paid much, but by and large it was a heap more than the usual renter ever saw in cash any other way. Papa held it was the fairest way to rent. Give a renter a chance to get ahead, if he was so minded, and left the farmer boss of his own land.

Silas Clark was buying his own place now, with what he'd saved and made renting from Papa. He'd built him up a right smart herd of milk cows, had a few head of sheep, and his woman had close to five hundred Rhode Island Red chickens that brought in considerable egg money. But Silas Clark was always a smart man. Worked hard to get ahead, and his family worked hard, too. He'd a pride in being a good renter, and Papa said Silas always went a little extra to make sure he was giving his money's worth. And when he'd done a good day's work for Papa, he'd turn to and work until in the night for himself.

Papa didn't look for Ben to be much account. He misput himself with Ben just to help Faleecy John. "Faleecy John's growing up," he said, "and he's too bright a boy to leave to Ben's careless ways. If he's taught to work right he'll make out better later in life. Maybe when he's grown he can save for himself and buy some land of his own." And that was what Faleecy John wanted, too. I know, for he told me so himself. The day they moved in.

It was a rainy, gray day in November the day they moved. No sun that morning. Just a thick, milky sky that seeped a fine, foggy mist onto the trees and bushes, and dripped in a dreary drizzle from the eaves. I watched all morning for their wagon, running in and out until Lucibel was fussed about the mud I kept tracking in. "I declare to goodness, Jeffie," she said, "I wish you'd simmer down! You can't make them come any quicker by flouncing around like a chicken with its head off! Just look at the kitchen floor!"

But I was too worked up to settle down. It sure was a big day for me!

It was along toward noon before I saw them coming down the road. I ran down to the gate and when the wagon passed I crawled on and rode the rest of the way with them. None of them said much, but I could tell Faleecy John was excited from the way he kept bouncing around. And the way he kept grinning at me.

The rent house was off the road a piece, down past the lower pasture out of sight of ours. It was a nice, white-painted little three-room house, with a picket fence all around, and the outbuildings out back. It was as good as many a ridge farmer ever owned for himself, for all it was a rent house, and as I've said, that was uncommon on the ridge. But Papa didn't hold with letting even a rent house go to wrack and ruin.

When they commenced unloading, their house plunder looked so bare and skimp it was pitiful. No real bedsteads and mattresses. No real tables and chairs. No stoves. Just make-do things, boxes and crates and stuff, and odds and ends of dishes and pots and pans. It hadn't looked so terrible over in the cabin to me. Or maybe I'd just got used to it there. But even I could tell it wasn't near going to fill three rooms, and that what they had was going to look out of place wherever they put it.

And it mortified and shamed Faleecy John. Not that he said anything. But he wouldn't look at me while we were helping with the unloading, and he kept whistling a tune that wasn't any tune at all. Like you will when you're trying to keep somebody from noticing. And as soon as we'd finished setting the stuff inside we ran off to the barn, glad to get away.

We propped our feet on the fence rail the way we'd seen the menfolks do and looked out over the pasture and Faleecy John chewed on a dry grass stalk, for all the world like Papa when he's thinking. Faleecy John looked all around . . . at the good land, and the good house, and the good barn and fencing, and he chewed on his stalk of grass and nodded his head. "Some day I want me a good farm, Jeffie. Like yer pa's. A good house an' buildings, cattle an' sheep an' horses. I'm aimin' to have 'em. I want the best of ever'thing. The best an' the nicest. That's fer me. I'm not fixin' to be a renter all my days, like Pa. Ain't no use in it, if yer willin' to work. An' I kin work as good as any. An' another thing," he said, spitting the grass stalk on the ground and turning toward me, "another thing. I ain't aimin' fer yore pa to lose none on this here rent deal. I know how Pa is. But I'm aimin' to see to it the work's done, an' done right. You kin tell yer pa that, too!"

I nodded my head wisely. I thought he was exactly right, and I didn't have any doubt at all but that he'd do just what he said he would, and that he would have everything he said he wanted. It made me proud to hear him talk.

Then we saw Lucibel coming down the path across the pasture. It had stopped raining, but on account of the damp she'd thrown a shawl over her head. She had on her old brown coat, which was too short for her, and underneath I could see she was wearing the yellow-sprigged dress. Of a rainy day she liked to wear the yellow dress. Said it made her feel like there was a little sunshine somewhere! I thought she looked more like a little girl than anything else, picking her way through the mud puddles in the path, not much taller than Faleecy John, now.

When he saw her Faleecy John reddened, and I knew before he spoke he was hating for her to see their old house things. But he stuck his chin up and turned toward the house. "We'll not allus have that old make-shift house plunder, either," he said, "come a day we'll have boughten stuff. Bedsteads an' cheers an' tables an' the like. I'm aimin' fer Ma to have 'em as soon as I kin make out to git 'em fer her."

I didn't know how to tell him I understood how he felt, so I said nothing. Just nodded again. And we waited for Lucibel to reach the barn lot. She was carrying a basket, and when she came through the gate she handed it to me. "I've brought Lydie some things," she said, "I allowed she wouldn't get around to doing much cooking today. And I've come to see if I can help."

We went to the house with her and Faleecy John called Lydie. I don't know what Lucibel had expected. As far as I know she'd never been in Lydie Squires' house. Doubtless she'd heard Granny tell how they lived but unless you see things like that with your own eyes it's hard to imagine how poor and shiftless it can be. I knew from the way her face looked she hadn't thought at all but what they had things to do with, same as others had. And I knew she was hard put to find anything to say at first.

Lydie pulled up one of the boxes for her to sit on, and wiped it off with her apron. She took the basket and set it on another box. "That's just some milk and butter, and a pie, Lydie," Lucibel said. "Moving's such a chore I knew in reason you wouldn't be having time to do much of anything else today, and I thought they'd come in handy.

Lydie mumbled something I couldn't hear, but Lucibel must of, for she nodded her head. "I came down a while yesterday," she went on, "to make sure the Clarks had left the place clean for you. Annie kept a good house, but moving sometimes gets things cluttered up."

"Hit's clean," Lydie said. She hadn't never sat down. Just stood by the door like she thought Lucibel would be leaving any time. She was gaunt and brown, her head covered by a faded old bonnet, and the black skirt she had on hooping the tops of her shoes in front and dragging the floor in the back. The leaders in her neck stood out like cords, and her mouth folded in over her snuff like a pocket. I was used to Lydie, but alongside of Lucibel that day she looked old and haggy and whipped out. Lucibel was pretty as a picture, and it came over me all at once that she ought never to be in the same room with Lydie. It was too unkind . . . it made the difference between them too plain.

"Is there anything I can do to help?" Lucibel asked.

I reckon even Lucibel knew that was a hopeless thing to ask. You could see there was nothing much even for Lydie to do. But it was only what any good neighbor offered to another, and Lucibel had come with goodness in her heart.

"I'll make out," Lydie said, and she went to the door to spit.

Lucibel ran a quick look around the room behind her back, and then she took a deep breath like she was gathering up her courage. "Lydie, if you wouldn't take it amiss, I've got some things in the storeroom up at the house maybe you could use. They're not doing me a bit of good, and just taking up room. I'd be glad to get them out of the way so's I could make better use of the room. There's a cookstove, and the kitchen cabinet I used before I got my new one, and there's two or three beds . . . " Her voice trailed off, running out and leaving stillness in the room.

I knew she was partly telling the truth, for Papa had just got her a new cookstove and kitchen cabinet the winter before. But she used the old ones in the wash house. Used the stove for canning in the summers, and for putting up her meat in the winter, and for boiling clothes when she washed, all the time. And she kept everything she worked with out there, in the kitchen cabinet. But it was like her to offer them, and make out herself the best she could. I didn't know of any extra beds we had, but I figured she'd take down the ones in the upstairs if need be.

But she might as well not have opened her mouth. For all Lydie said was, "We'll make out."

Lucibel turned pink and she licked her tongue over her lips. "Well . . . " she said, "I just thought I'd . . . well, I thought maybe . . . "

Lydie didn't come right out and say they didn't want none of her charity, but she might as well of. She just looked at Lucibel and said again they'd make out.

Lucibel stood up then and held her hand out to me. "Well, we'd better go. I'm just keeping you from your work, and doubtless Jeffie gets in the way, too." And with her head high she walked out the door. Me with her.

Granny was home when we got there. She was heating up the coffee, it being so chill and damp outside. She looked at Lucibel over her specks and then she got down another cup from the dish cabinet. She poured it full and pushed it across the table. "Set down," she said, "an' drink yer coffee. You want some?" she grinned at me.

"Now, Mama, I don't like for Jeffie to have coffee!"

"Hit won't hurt him," Granny said and she went right on getting down another cup. It didn't do a bit of good to cross Granny. She just plowed right on her way. I put cream and sugar in it and took it over to the little table by the window where I'd left the book I was reading. I thought I loved coffee the best of anything in the world. Reckon mostly it was because I couldn't have it often. But I was sure proud Granny was there that day, and I hovered over that cup of coffee determined to make it last quite a time.

Doubtless Granny and Lucibel forgot I was even in the room. I paid no heed to what they were saying for a spell, but directly the words seemed more important. I've taken notice more than once that you can read or be busy with your own thoughts and folks can talk right across your head and you won't hear what they're saying so long as they're talking even and calm and level-like. But let anger or fear or feeling of any sort come into their voices, and the words suddenly drop around you like spears or arrows, and you can't make sense of your reading, or think your own thoughts any longer. You must pay heed to the words and the feelings behind them. They prickle the air like electricity and they prickle your own feelings like they'd found their way under your skin.

Lucibel's voice was angry now. "It was a foolish thing, doubtless, to offer the things. But she needn't have been so proud and haughty refusing them. I only meant well!"

And Granny's voice was dry. "Hit was an uncommon foolish thing to do. They ain't nobody so low but has got their own kind of pride. An' Lydie's is special, as you should ort to know better than ary other person."

"But, Mama, they've not got anything. I tell you, they haven't even got a stove to cook on. Or a bed to sleep in!"

"You needn't to tell me what they've not got. I've saw with my own eyes. Don't fergit I've birthed ever' youngun they ever had."

"I know. But it just came over me how pitiful it was. And I was ashamed to have so much."

"If you didn't have ary thing in this world but Mark Harbin you'd have more'n Lydie's got, an' well you know it."

Granny got up to pour more coffee. Lucibel stirred hers slowly, and she propped her chin in the palm of her hand. "Mama," she said after a time, sort of soft and dreamy-like, "was Lydie pretty when she was younger?"

Granny grunted. "Cain't you remember?"

"How would I remember? Lydie is twenty years older than me. She was already grown and married to Ben Squires when I was born!"

Granny pushed her specks up on her head. "I allus mislay the years someways. I've got so used to you an' Mark bein' married I fergit you're another generation from him an' Lydie an' Ben an' them. No, she wasn't to say purty. Never was, in my opinion. But she had sperrit, an' she loved to go an' have fun. She was light-hearted an' light-footed, too. It's the years with Ben has made her look the way she does. The years, an' the sourness of knowin' what she could of had, stacked up agin what she got. That's what's eat into her an' ganted her up an' give her the sharp tongue she's got. I reckon hit would gravel any woman to live the way she's had to live, an' look across here at you an' Mark an' know hit might of been her." Granny saucered her coffee and blew on it. "You ain't wearyin' none about her, are ye?"

"No. I've not ever worried none about her. I reckon

I begrudge her all those years Mark loved her and wouldn't look at another woman. I reckon you could say I begrudge her them."

"You wouldn't of been married to him today if he hadn't of."

Lucibel laughed. "That's right. So I needn't even begrudge her them."

Granny sucked in her coffee noisily. "You've come to think a heap of him, haven't you? Even if you wasn't so certain at the time?"

Lucibel stood up and took her empty cup to the cook table. "I love him better than life itself."

"Well, don't be thinkin' Mark's rentin' to Ben is on account of Lydie, then. Fer it ain't."

Lucibel's head went up proudly. "I know why he's renting to Ben," she said, "he's renting to Ben because I asked him to. On account of Faleecy John, that's why."

Granny went humph in her coffee and there was quiet for a time. The next they spoke was of the early frost and whether the late beans were killed.

The prickles went out of the air and the voices went flat and even and calm again, and the words they said were meaningless. I went back to my reading. I can tell you now that it was page sixty-five of *Swiss Family Robinson*.

# eleven

LUCIBEL made me wait until after dinner to go see
Faleecy John the next day. She said maybe I'd be in
the way. I told her it was a fair day and we'd play outside, but she made me wait just the same.

When I got there Faleecy John was ricking up cook
wood in the corner of the yard. I pitched in to help. I
like to rick wood. It makes a clean, straight stack, and
I like the laying of the pieces just so. Faleecy John
would pitch the sticks over to me and I'd stack them.
It went smooth and easy, and the sun was warm on our
backs.

We had it almost done when Silas Clark pulled
around the corner of the house in his spring wagon. He
had his oldest girl with him. Jenny, that was. I'd seen

102

her many a time around the place when I'd come with Papa, but she was a lot older than me and I'd never paid her any mind. I reckon she was getting close to fifteen by now.

She was a right pretty girl, in a plump partridgey sort of way. Fact is, as she sat there shy and modest-like on the wagon seat with her head down and her eyes drooped, that's what she reminded me most of. She had that same swollen, pouter breast, smooth-rounded and high, for all the world like a little hen partridge. Her hair was brown and her skin was brown, and when she lifted her eyes finally, they were brown, too.

Silas got down and went in the house and left her sitting there. Faleecy John edged over towards the wagon and I followed. "Howdy, Jenny," I said when we came up to the wheel. "You all forget something when you moved?"

"Howdy," she said, and her voice was whispery and low, like she was too timid to talk out, and while she spoke to me, it was Faleecy John she looked at.

He spoke then. "Howdy, Jenny."

An it was like his eyes, suddenly black and glistening, wouldn't turn loose of hers, their look held so long.

"You all forget something?" I asked again, impatiently.

Jenny slid her eyes over to me and she shook her head. "No. But Pa couldn't take ever'thing the day we moved, so we left some stuff up in the loft room. We've come for it."

"Whyn't you git down?" Faleecy John said.

She shook her head. "I better hadn't."

"Why? C'mon!"

The smooth, rounded front of her dress lifted with her indrawn breath. But she still shook her head.

Faleecy John wheeled away. "Oh well," he said indifferently, "Jeffie an' me was jist goin' out to the barn to see the pups. It's no matter if you don't want to see 'em. C'mon, Jeffie."

And he sauntered carelessly off toward the barn lot. "Ps-s-t," he hissed in my ear, "git the pups in that box on the porch an' run around the other way an' put 'em in the barn!"

I ducked around the end of the wagon, and as I ran I saw Jenny crawling over the wagon wheel. I didn't blame her. I'd want to see the pups, too!

I grabbed the box from the end of the porch, skirted the house and cut across behind the chicken house to the barn. I didn't know whether Faleecy John wanted them left in the box or not, but I thought they'd show up better if they weren't, so I dug a little nest in some loose hay in a stall and dumped them out in it. Oh, they were beautiful pups! And my little tan fellow was the prettiest of all. I picked him up and rubbed my face against him, and he was as soft as Lucibel's hair. Just another month, now, and I could take him home. But I could see him every day now that he lived so close.

I was cuddling him and petting him when Faleecy John and Jenny came in. She had a fit over all of them. She got down on her knees and picked them up and petted them, and talked soft and sweet to them.

"This un's Jeffie's," Faleecy John said, motioning to Snooper in my arms.

"Let me hold him," she begged, and she took him and rubbed her face against him just like I'd done. "He's the purtiest one of all," she said, and I swelled with pride. I decided Jenny had pretty good sense, after all. To recognize such a good dog like that.

"Yeah," Faleecy John said, and then to me, "Lucibel seen him yit?"

I was taking him back from Jenny. "No."

"Whyn't you take him an' show him to her?"

"Now?"

"Shore."

I flew out the door and down the path across the pasture, the pup snuggled in my arms. Papa was at the house, too, and he allowed he'd never seen a finer dog! Lucibel held him in her lap, and when he wet on her she never said a word, just laughed. Papa laughed, too, and scolded a little. "You'll have to housebreak him, son," he warned, when he handed him back to me.

"He's not going to be any house dog!" I said scornfully, "This one's going to be the best fox hound in the hills!"

"I wouldn't be surprised," Papa agreed, and Lucibel nodded her head along with ours.

"What you going to name him?" she asked, rubbing her finger down his back.

"Snooper," I said, "on account of he's going to snoop out rabbits and coons and possums and foxes."

Papa said he thought that was a fine name, but I'd better take him back to his mother now.

I was so pleased that Papa and Lucibel liked the pup that when I got near the barn I started yelling at Faleecy John. "Hey," I screamed, "hey, Faleecy John! Papa was at the house and he got to see Snooper, too. And they both think he's fine. Hey!"

I skidded to a stop in the aisle of the barn, raising a dust and puffing for breath. Jenny and Faleecy John were still watching the rest of the pups. I put Snooper down with the others, and Jenny stood up and turned toward the door. "I better go," she said, the words breathy and husky in her throat. She slewed a look at Faleecy John, and then at me, and her neck got red as fire. We all started out the door, and when we got outside she walked off toward the house.

"Hey, Jenny," I called without thinking when I noticed, "You got hay in your hair!"

She wheeled around and looked sharp at me. "Shut up," she snapped, but her hand went to the back of her head just the same. She pulled the wisp of hay out of her hair and the red in her neck went clean up her face to her forehead. Besides, her face took on a funny look, scared and startled. She turned quickly and fled to the wagon and crawled up on the seat, like she hadn't ever left it.

It puzzled me and gave me a queer feeling. And then all at once I knew why Faleecy John wanted Jenny to get down, and why he wanted the pups in the barn. And why he had sent me to show Snooper to Lucibel. I knew, and it made me sick at my stomach and scared and afraid of something dark and ugly and slimy. Worse, it made me not like Faleecy John. It was like he had changed some way. Like he wasn't quite the same person.

"You oughtn't," I said. "It's not nice to . . . little girls . . . " but my tongue got hung in the roof of my mouth and I couldn't go on.

Faleecy John was standing with his hands in his pockets, the toe of his shoe drawing circles in the mud in the barn yard. He looked up when I started talking, and the only other time I had ever seen him look so tense and still was that day we had seen the bull down in the pasture. His eyes were just as black and just as shining, and though it was November there was a fine bead of sweat around his mouth. He took one of his hands out of his pocket and it was shaking when he wiped the sweat off his face. He frightened me. Just looking at him like that frightened me terribly.

"The hell it's not nice!" he said, then, and he laughed. "Besides, she's a big girl now. An' I'm gettin' to be a big boy." He looked across the lot at Jenny sitting on the wagon seat, eyes demurely dropped, swollen pouter breast chaste under her smooth dress front, and he laughed again. "Jesus! Who'd have thought Jenny Clark . . . !"

But I didn't want to hear any more. I went home, and he was still looking at Jenny Clark and chuckling when I left.

He wanted everything, Faleecy John. He wanted it all. The best. The nicest. The most. The worst. All of it. It was all too good to waste.

# twelve

**B**UT OF COURSE I didn't stay mad with Faleecy John long. Couldn't anybody ever, as far as I knew. I've known men to cuss him up one side and down the other, madder than a wet hen at him, and laugh with him over it next day. He'd a way of acting like nothing had ever happened, of meeting you warm and easy-like, that took the wind right out of your sails. You can't stay mad with a man that won't let you. Not that I ever wanted to. For I was always too glad to ease the storm that stirred in me when things went wrong betwixt us. So, when he came by the next morning wanting to go walnut-picking, it was like the sun had shafted through the clouds. The chunked knot in my stomach dissolved and the lead weight in my chest lifted.

It was good that first year they rented from us. Ben sort of surprised Papa by working and making out a right good hand. He was always good in timber and there was a piece of woods Papa had been aiming to cut over for quite a spell. Ben took it over that winter and Papa said he hadn't ever seen a smarter piece of work. And Faleecy John helped a lot, evenings and Saturdays. That was his last year of school. He'd finish up the eighth grade come February, and that was as far as ridge folks ever went. If that far. Some didn't get beyond the fourth or fifth. Just the Harbins ever went off for more schooling.

Faleecy John was eager to get through, so's he could take a man's part in the work. He was always a good worker. And willing. He didn't to say like all kinds of work. For he disliked the tedious tending of crops. It went too slow for him. But he did whatever came to hand to do, and did it well. Mainly, though, he liked working with the teams . . . plowing, hauling, harvesting. Anything to do with the horses, he liked. And was extra good at.

The bay mare that Papa had bought was just the same as his. He had all the care of her, and Papa had given him leave to ride her any time he liked. Nobody else ever drove or rode her but Faleecy John. She had his mark on her, and he kept her curried and combed until her coat was like satin.

Papa had given me the chestnut when it was still a leggy, gawky colt. But he had grown into a beautiful horse by now, and I wouldn't have traded him for ten like the bay mare. But it was good for us both to have a horse we thought such a heap of. Faleecy John turned his nose up at the chestnut, and I looked down on the mare, but that was just in fun. By and large I reckon they were about evenly matched. The mare was faster, but my chestnut had more wind. We had some fine rides on them, both then and later.

Faleecy John had his thirteenth birthday that December and Lucibel baked him a cake and put candles on it. They shone as bright as stars in a dark sky when she lit them that evening. "Make a wish, Faleecy John," she said, laughing across the table at him. "Make a wish and blow. Blow hard, and if you blow them all out, your wish will come true."

"Fer shore?"

"For sure!"

He must have known what he wanted to wish, for he didn't once stop to think. He just stooped and blew one strong breath, and all the bright flames winked out. All of them. And the cake was dark without them. When he raised his head Faleecy John looked at Lucibel. "You said fer shore," he said.

"Unless you wished for the moon," she laughed back at him.

And where he was holding on to the back of the chair Faleecy John's hands knuckled white. A shiver ran down my back and raised the hairs on my neck. I looked around, thinking Papa had left the door open and a cold wind was blowing in. But the door was closed tight, and Papa was standing over by the fireplace, his pipe curling a cloud of smoke around his head. He looked tall and steady standing there, and the cold went away. I laughed at my foolishness. Papa wouldn't never have left a door open. He was always careful about things like that.

Then nothing would do but Lucibel must have Faleecy John line up against the wall so she could mark off how tall he was. Five foot four, I recollect. Just one

inch shorter than her. She said she reckoned it wouldn't
be long before she'd have to commence looking up at
him. No doubts about it, he was shooting up fast those
days. Growing right out of his clothes. His overhalls
were always too short for him, and his arms bean-poled
out of his sleeves. He was lean as a scantling, but broad-
ening already in the shoulders. His face was fuzzing
over a little, and sometimes when he talked his voice
would crack. He was proud of growing up. You could
see it when he stood there letting Lucibel measure him.
He squared his chin up to make his head as tall as he
could, and Papa laughed at him and said he looked like
a young cock rooster.

Just for fun, then, Lucibel made Papa and me line
up and be measured. She had to stand on a chair for
Papa. He was six foot two. And me . . . well, I did
well to pass the five-foot mark. I reckon I knew even
then I wasn't ever going to be as tall as Papa, and I
wanted to, in the worst way.

Lucibel put her arm around my shoulder and said,
"You'll have to let Papa and Faleecy John be the biggest
right now. But you'll catch up with them some day.
Besides, I need somebody my size around here a little
longer."

It made me feel some better. But not much.

Lucibel cut the cake then, and we ate it, with some
of her spiced peaches and cream. And then Papa gave
Faleecy John his present. I was as surprised as Faleecy
John, for hadn't anybody said a word to me about it.
And it was the first time ever we gave him a present,
too. I figured Papa was afraid I'd give it away if I'd
known, which likely I would of.

It was a gun. A brand-new .22, and Faleecy John's
eyes like to popped out of his head when he saw it.

Papa showed him all about it, for all Faleecy John had
ever handled before was Ben's old muzzle-loading shotgun. He listened careful-like to what Papa told him,
and you could tell by the way he held it and handled
it he prized it a heap and was prouder than Jupiter to
have it.

I reached over to run my hand down the stock, it
looked so smooth and shiny. And Papa looked at me
and said real quick, "You'll get one just like it when
you're twelve, Jeffie."

Lucibel laughed sort of trembly-like. "Is everybody
going to grow up and be big men around here, and
leave me with no little boys?"

"Jist as quick as we kin," Faleecy John promised, and
he sighted down the gun barrel, making out he was
drawing a bead on a squirrel.

We went hunting a heap that winter. It was a white
winter with deep snows and the rabbits were thick.
Faleecy John let me shoot his gun sometimes, but
mostly I just went along. I was content to wait for my
own gun.

We had us a trapline and every evening when we got
home from school we ran it. We mostly caught musk-
rats. Their pelts brought a right smart price those days,
and Faleecy John was wanting to make all the money
he could. He was saving every penny he could get. He
was going to buy Lydie a real bedstead when he got
enough.

But we had work to do, too. There was corn to be
ground, and the stock to be fed, and wood to be sawed
and split. Night and morning we had to help with the
milking, and we thought Lucibel used more water than
anybody in the world! Looked like we'd draw the well
dry some days.

When spring came on we had to help in the tobacco, for we still set by hand on the ridge. Faleecy John had been helping Ben for several years, but it was my first time, and backbreaking work it was, too. If you can think of anything more tedious than crawling along a row on your hands and knees, digging little holes in the ground, pouring in a dab of water then sticking a tobacco plant in and firming the earth around it, I'd like for you to name it. And we had ten acres that year! That was before the government took over and told every farmer how much he could plant. Everybody grew what he could handle. And none of it brought very much. But you wouldn't think of not having a tobacco crop on the ridge, even if you didn't more than break even. Nowadays I've got a three-acre base, but it brings me six or eight times as much as Papa used to make on ten or fifteen acres.

After the tobacco and corn are out in the spring there's a little lull in farm work until the crops have grown enough to work. We went fishing, then. Not down in the pond, but clean down to Little Lost Creek. Many's the hour we've sat on the bank in the sun with our reed poles in our hands, and a big, fat red worm on the end of our hooks. And many was the mess of crappie and bream and sun perch we'd bring home with us.

And when summer came on and the water got low and warm, in that same hole where we fished Faleecy John taught me to swim. I don't know when or how he learned himself. As far back as I could remember he'd always gone swimming, and it was some of those times when he'd slipped off to the creek before Lucibel would let me go that had left me feeling the lonesomest without him. I'd begged him it's unknowing the times to let me go with him. But he wouldn't hardly ever do anything that he knew would worry Lucibel, and he never would take me.

But one day along after my birthday in June we started out with our fishing poles, and like he'd just thought of it he turned around and told Lucibel, "I'm aimin' to start learnin' Jeffie how to swim today."

I thought she'd raise a fuss, sure, but all she did was nod her head and say, "Be careful."

She stood in the door and watched us clean out of sight, though, and I walked extra tall and swaggery as far as she could see, for I was proud she knew I was growing up, too.

There wasn't much teaching to it after all. Or maybe it was because Faleecy John could tell a thing so simple it was easy. And maybe it was because with Faleecy John telling me, I wasn't scared at all. We stripped and waded in and he told me if I'd just unlimber and let go I couldn't sink if I wanted to, and would just float on top the water like a piece of wood. He stood and watched me while I tried it, and when I floated as light and easy as a cork he laughed and told me to turn over and start paddling. That's all there was to it, but I felt as big as the biggest fish in the creek doing it. I don't reckon I'd take any prizes swimming, from Faleecy John's teaching, but I reckon I'd be mighty hard to drown at that.

# thirteen

IT WENT queer and strange to be going back to school in July without Faleecy John. It was like I had been divided in two, and part of me was going to school and the other part staying at home. Worst of it was I knew this was the beginning of a difference that would last a spell, for I knew I'd have to go off to school for three or four years when I got through with the ridge school. And in a way I wanted to go. I wanted to keep on reading and learning. I knew I wouldn't be satisfied to stop where I was. But in another way I hated it. For I was afraid things would never be the same for me and Faleecy John again.

All summer I had been dreading the opening day of school, trying to push it away from me. But it came, like all things we dread, and I had to start off down the

road alone. I hadn't ever made close friends with anybody else at school. There were plenty of cousins, big
and little, and I had got along well enough with all the
other boys. It was just that as long as Faleecy John was
there nobody else mattered much to me.   He was
enough. So I made a bad time of it the first few days.

And then, like the things we dread usually turn out,
it wasn't so bad any more. Mostly that was on account
of Jolie Turner, the little girl that had called crybaby
at me the first day of school. I'd forgot that long ago,
and as much as girls and boys are ever friends at that
age, I'd counted her a friend. She was in my grade and
I'd helped her with her arithmetic, and she'd helped
me with spelling. I'd always thought she was pretty and
cute, and Faleecy John had teased me some about her
being my girl. But I reckon she didn't actually come to
be my girl until he wasn't going to school any longer.
She didn't take the place of Faleecy John, but she
helped fill the gap his not being there made.

The kids teased me about her a heap, for we took to
eating our dinners together . . . her and me and Ida
Stone, who was her best friend. But by the time I'd
licked several of them there wasn't anything more said.
Not that I stuck around her all the time, for I didn't.
I played ball or pitched horseshoes, or run foot races
as much as any of the rest of them. But we ate together
every day, and I moved my seat over next to hers, and
I'd pack her books as far as she went up the holler.
And inside of me I called her my girl, even if I did lick
the others for saying so.

She reminded me some of Lucibel, with her yellow
braids and and white skin. Only Lucibel's eyes were
greeny-gold, and Jolie's were as blue as the skies. She
had tempery ways, though, and sometimes I felt like I

was in a pot of water with it boiling, for no good reason that I could see. She'd flare up over something, maybe just me helping Ida with her arithmetic, and fly off the handle and not speak the rest of the day. Or she'd take a spell of letting someone else pack her books for her. But she'd always get over it in a little while and be merry and laughing again.

Ida Stone lived next house from Jolie's down on Little Lost Creek, and they were always together just like me and Faleecy John. I never thought much about her one way or the other. She was always there, plain brown hair and brown eyes to match, kind of quiet, but I remember noticing once there was a little dimple tucked in the corner of her mouth. You couldn't see it most times. But when she laughed it sort of flashed out and lit up her whole face and made it look different. After that sometimes I'd try to make her laugh just to watch it dart out and in again. But I don't recollect I ever packed her books for her so much as one time. You never thought of such with Ida. She was quiet, but she wasn't what you'd call serious. I reckon mostly you'd say she just minded her own business with no foolishness about her. And while she was best friends with Jolie, Jolie never could run over her. When Jolie blew hot and cold Ida just paid her no mind and went on. Soon or late Jolie'd make up just like she did with me. As far as I ever thought about it, I liked Ida Stone. But it was Jolie I liked best and named my girl.

It was along late in the fall that year that Faleecy John and I had our second fight. And there was no doubt he licked me good and proper. Work was caught up at home and he'd come to school with me that day, just to visit. I was proud and happy to have him there and had showed off considerable in front of him, winning all the foot races and pitching my best in the ball game at noon. It sure was a big day.

We'd started home and as usual I was packing Jolie's books and her and Ida were walking with us up the holler. Faleecy John got to picking at Jolie and chasing her, making out like he was going to pull her hair, and they ran on up the path. Ran quite a piece ahead and out of sight. When we came around a bend in the path, Faleecy John had her pinned against a tree and was kissing her.

Ida stopped still and I heard her draw in her breath. But I never stopped at all. I was so mad I was blind with it, and without even thinking to put Jolie's books down I charged at him. I heard her squeal when I flung him around, but that was all, for I was too mad to hear or think anything more.

It was a good fight while it lasted. And while he licked me, he had a split lip and a bloody nose to show for it. When we picked ourselves up Jolie had gone. Scared, I reckon. But Ida was still standing there. She handed me my cap that had fallen off and that she'd been holding, and she looked at Faleecy John level and straight. But she didn't say a word to either one of us. Just went on ahead of us to where the trails forked, and then she took the lefthand fork to where she lived, without ever looking back.

The fight had taken all the mad out of me. It had boiled up fierce and sudden, but now it was gone, and I felt cleaned out and fine. But I thought there ought to be something more to it. It oughtn't just to end, up in the air, like. So I said to Faleecy John, "Don't do it again. Jolie's my girl. Just don't forget that!"

Faleecy John just grinned at me and brushed the leaves off his coat. He started up the trail, but he looked back once over his shoulder. "She liked it," he said.

# fourteen

THAT WAS the fall, too, that Ben commenced slacking off on his work. He'd been doing fine, but seemed like with Faleecy John at home now he left more and more of it up to him, and he started going back over to Lo and Behold.

And Papa was worried. Not that he said anything. But you could tell from the still look on his face most any time, and the way he'd look clean through you sometimes when you were talking, like his mind was a thousand miles away. He thinned down some, too, which he could ill afford, him being built on the gaunt side the way he was. He wasn't puny, and when Lucibel would ask him if he felt bad he'd always say no, but he had the uneasy look of a man not knowing what was coming next. Which doubtless he didn't, with Ben drinking again and sulling and leaving the work to Faleecy John.

Seemed like we all got creepy and jumpy, Lucibel being worried about Papa the way she was, and me being scared Ben'd commence on Faleecy John again, and Papa trying to keep up the work, and Faleecy John honing down trying to do his part. Even the elements were dreary, it being a windy, rainy fall with no color to the woods, and a heavy load of fog and mist day after day. It was a dismal and tiresome time.

The first cold snap came on a Saturday right after Thanksgiving and Papa said we'd kill the first of the hogs. He sent me to get Granny to help Lucibel with the lard and sausage, and he went down to tell Ben and Faleecy John.

Granny lived about a mile away, and I reckon it took about an hour, walking over there, waiting for her to get ready, and the two of us walking back. And when we got there Lucibel was helping Papa into the kitchen. His face was mashed into a bloody pulp and his clothes were torn and muddy. His knuckles were skinned and one thumb was split wide open. And his eyes had a queer, glazed look.

"He and Ben had a fight," Lucibel said to Granny. "Get some water ready while I go after some clean rags." She swished past us and ran out of the room.

Granny poured water into the dishpan from the tea-kettle and set it on the table. She went to stripping Papa's shirt off. His shoulders were cut from the rocks where he'd rolled, and he jumped when her hands touched them. When she'd got his shirt off she laid it on the table and came around to stand in front of him.

"He knows?" she said, and the sound of her voice

was as dull and flat as the plunk of water-logged wood.

Papa nodded his head and leaned his arms on the table, putting his hands over his face.

"What did he want?"

"Fifty acres of bottom land."

Granny put her hand on his shoulder and he lifted his face and looked at her. "Monnie, there was just that one time . . . just once . . . "

Granny's name was Monica, and those that didn't call her Granny always called her Monnie. Not many did, just Papa and one or two others that were older. She kept her hand on his shoulder, but her face was gentle. "Once is all it takes, Mark," and she sort of laughed.

"I know . . . but so long ago. Before Lucibel . . . you know that, don't you?"

"Shore. I kin add."

"And I didn't know. I didn't know!"

"No."

There was a stillness in the room: I was afraid to move. I knew they had forgotten me, and like a person caught eavesdropping I felt guilty and ashamed, but I didn't know what to do. What they were saying didn't make sense to me, but I knew they'd forgotten I was there or they wouldn't be talking so. But not knowing what to do I just stood still where I was, feeling tight and sick and scared.

"What am I going to do, Monnie?" There was a roughness in Papa's voice that made me want to cry. A roughness and a sadness that I'd never heard before. It made me want to put my arms around him and tell him not to worry. I'd help. Lucibel would help. Granny would help. We'd all help, whatever it was. It wasn't his to carry alone. He needn't to worry so. "What am

I going to do?" he said again, and he dropped his head on the table.

Granny rubbed her hand against his head like he was a little boy. She stood there and smoothed his hair and looked at him gentle and soft-like. And then her face went gray and harsh, and she took her hand away. "They ain't but one thing *to* do," she said, and she went to the window and stood looking out at the frostbitten pasture. "They ain't but one thing to do."

And then Lucibel made a clatter coming down the hall and Papa squared himself around in the chair and Granny stirred to put the kettle on the fire. And I let my breath out easy and sat down. It was like an iron fist had been squeezing my chest and it hurt when it let go.

# fifteen

AFTER THAT we didn't see much of Ben, and I reckon none of us missed him. The fight was never named. It was like it hadn't been, so far as talk of it was concerned. But the knowledge of it lay there and made us all uneasy. Lucibel felt most to blame for having persuaded Papa into renting to Ben, and she worried about it some, until Papa told her to hush. Said likely he would have done so anyhow. But that didn't any way mend what was done or help Papa decide what to do next. Ben was like a cloud over us, for all we didn't go around him, or him come around us.

Faleecy John said he didn't stay at home much either. Looked like he was always over at Lo and Behold getting drunk, or laying on the bed sleeping it off when he was at home. Certain it is he never laid his hand to do any part of the work again. Faleecy John took over all that would have been his part. He and Papa snugged the farm down for the winter. They got in the fodder and the corn, strengthened the fences, sawed and split and ricked up the wood, and made ready for the cold. I did my part after school and on Saturdays.

Winter closed in early that year. Long before Christmas we were frozen in. Winter on the ridge is always harsh . . . a time of being housebound more or less, with raw, cold rains driving out of the north, keen, high winds lashing at the house corners, and frost hardening the earth to a brittle metal. But if you've made ready for it, it can be a pleasant time, too. I never minded, once school was out, for it gave me a snug, warm feeling to sit before a roaring fire with a good book to read, listening to the wind and the rain and the sleet beating against the roof, knowing it couldn't touch me.

But that winter was different. It was partly the knowledge of Ben, and the uneasiness that hung over us, but the winter was a terrible burden in itself. It was like the elements had set out to persecute the ridge. Besides the early cold there was a lot of sickness . . . colds and grippe and the like. Lydie came down with a chill and fever just before Christmas, and the first time she laid on the new bedstead Faleecy John had got her was the night she took sick. But she was mighty proud of it, and she said it was a God's blessing to have it when her bones were aching until they felt like they were coming unjointed.

Lucibel *would* go and do for her, knowing how helpless a household is when a woman's sick. There's no place in the world where a woman is as sorely needed as in the country. Let the woman of a house get sick, and it just goes to pieces. In the city, now, a man can make out very well. There's restaurants and laundries and such, and he can eat and keep his clothes clean all right. But in the country he makes a poor out of it when the hub of the house comes down.

Just about the time Lydie was up and around again, Lucibel came down with it. And it was our house went to pieces. Granny came, of course. Not only to do for Papa and me, but to take care of Lucibel. For Papa was always scared out of his wits when anything happened to her. All he could do was fuss and twitch and wander back and forth through the house.

"Lord, Mark," Granny said to him, "You've got her dead and buried! She's jist got a chill an' fever. Don't amount to nothin'. Quit pesterin' her askin' how she feels! Leave her be so she kin sleep an' git some rest! You'd wear a well person out, pacin' around like a nervy cat. Git out an' work outside a while."

Just Granny's fussiness made you feel better. For me and Faleecy John were almost as bad as Papa, and she drove us all out and scolded and fumed at us until we couldn't help laughing. She was just like a little old banty hen I used to have that squawked and ruffled her feathers every time anybody came near!

Seemed like Faleecy John was more worried over Lucibel than he had been over his own mother. "Ma has allus been pore an' stringy," is the way he put it, "but she's stout fer all that, an' seemed like I knowed she'd be all right in time. But Lucibel's so leetle an' delicate . . . looks like hit wouldn't take but a fair wind to blow her clean away."

Lucibel's being sick was the reason Faleecy John didn't have a cake for his birthday. She was able to sit

up and Granny would let us in her room by then, but
she was too weak to be on her feet.

"I aimed to bake you one every year, Faleecy John,"
she told him the day before, "just like I do Jeffie, but
I'll have to miss this year looks like."

Granny sniffed. "I'll bake him one if you're so set
on it."

Lucibel and Faleecy John both spoke at the same
time. "No . . ." and then they laughed. "You first,"
Lucibel said.

Faleecy John ducked his head, "Well, I jist wouldn't
want her to trouble."

"That's what I was going to say, too," Lucibel said.
"You've got your hands full without extra baking,
Mama."

Granny smoothed down her apron. "Reckon a leetle
cake wouldn't put me out none."

But Lucibel said no, and Granny left it lay.

The next morning Faleecy John came to the house
and he had a box wrapped in pink crêpe paper for Lucibel. "Hit's my birthday," he said, "but I'm givin' you
the present!"

"Why, Faleecy John!" Lucibel said, laughing and
trying to unwrap the box all at the same time. Her fingers were so shaky they got caught in the strings and we
had to help her at the last. When she got the box open
it was a little muff made of soft, gray rabbit skins. It
was just big enough for her two hands, and made so it
was puffy and round, and it was lined with some sort
of silky stuff.

She held it up to her face and rubbed her cheek
against it. And I could see her eyes were wet. She
dashed the tears away. "This fever has made me so
weak I cry over nothing," she fussed. "It's beautiful,

Faleecy John! Just beautiful! Where did you get it?"

"Trapped the rabbits an' had a woman over at the county seat make the skins up. I don't know whether she done a good job or not, but folks said she was right good at it."

"She couldn't have done better! It's perfect! And think how warm it'll keep my hands when I go out this winter!"

"I'm glad you like it. I hoped you would. I was goin' to give it to you Christmas, but seein' you're sick an' all I got to thinkin' hit might make a good birthday present."

Papa came in then, and Lucibel passed the muff around so we could all feel of it and admire it. It sure was pretty, and that's a fact. Granny made a pot of coffee and cut some gingerbread and we had a right nice birthday party for Faleecy John after all. Seemed like he was more pleased to be giving a present than to be getting one.

As if the cold and sickness weren't enough that winter, it set in to rain right after the new year turned, and it rained for twenty-six days straight. Some days it would pour down hard, drowning the fields and the pastures and sluicing the yards with gullies of fast-flowing water. Other days it would turn to a cold, freezing drizzle that iced over as fast as it fell, turning the trees slick and black and bending their branches low under the weight of it. Either way it was rain that kept falling, and the roads turned to a mush of mud that even a mule had hard work to get through. School had to let out a month early, and I was glad not to have to plod through the mud and the weather.

We had got up plenty of wood that fall, so the fires were kept roaring and the house stayed warm and dry in spite of the damp. But it was dark enough inside most days to burn a lamp at noon. The houses here on the ridge are built low-ceilinged. A man can lay the flat of his hand against the ceiling without stretching, and while the space above makes for a cool house in the summer, and a warm one in the winter, it does make it mighty dark when the sun don't shine.

It was a bad time for Lucibel, who never could abide dark, rainy days even when she was well, and seemed like when she got up from the grippe she was twitchy and cross an awful lot. Granny said the grippe left you feeling like that . . . nervy and restless.

Lucibel loved the sun, anyhow, and a whole month of dark and rain frashed her so that she was fussy as an old wet hen. We had the chores to do, bringing in wood, milking, drawing water and such, and it meant muddy boot tracks every time we stepped inside. She scolded at us for tracking up the floors, and kept a broom swishing at our heels all the time. And the floor wouldn't much more than dry from one scrubbing until she was at it again. "Just like a pigpen," she'd say, running for the mop and fretting, "just like living in a pigpen!"

And she fussed at us for hanging our wet coats and caps around the kitchen stove to dry. Said she couldn't cook a pot of soup without having a cap or a mitten fall in. But they had to dry, and behind the kitchen stove was the warmest place to hang them. Even when she fussed, though, she made sure they were good and dry before we put them on again.

She would sit at the window with her mending, not touching the mending but just sitting there looking out across the dreary, water-soaked land, and it was like it had all soaked into her turning her gray and heavy with it. I'd hear her sigh sometimes, and then she'd flounce out and make a cake, or pop some corn, or something to pass the time.

She'd get out her yellow dress and put it on, day after day, until finally one day she threw it back in a corner of her closet and said she was sick of making like she was the sun itself. Said in her opinion the sun had gone clean to the other side of the world and didn't ever intend to come back. Said there wasn't any use pretending she felt gay and shiney when she never!

Faleecy John laughed at her and said she'd better cover her head then, for her yellow hair was bright as the sun, and as far as his need went, was sufficient until the real thing took a notion to show itself again. He could nearly always get her to laugh, but he didn't come very often now. Once or twice a week was all. He was put to it to keep wood up for Lydie, and to take care of their animals. Ben was hardly ever sober any more.

Papa was worried when the rains kept on. Said if they didn't let up there'd be floods down in the valley sure. And he was right. For when the rains started in the third week, Little Lost Creek went out on a rampage, spreading itself all over the bottoms. Folks that never in all their time had been endangered by high waters had to be brought out by boats, leaving their houses and barns sticking up out of the wide sea of water like little islands. We could stand on the ledge at the top of the holler and look down in the valley, and as far as you could see was a swirling, sullen width of water. Papa shook his head over it and said he'd never seen the like. It was a bad time for the valley folks.

How it happened that the cattle in the back pasture broke through we didn't know. And the worst was they broke through the fence that run along the edge of the holler. Probably on account of the ground being so soft and water-soaked the fenceposts gave way, we reckoned. But break through they did. They were beef cattle and we didn't bring them up to the barns near the house. There was a shelter built up there in the pasture for them and Papa usually went to see about them every two or three days. He came tearing in that day and said the fence was down and the cattle were gone down the holler. "Go get Ben and Faleecy John," he told me, "I'll go on ahead. Come down the holler, for I've seen their tracks that way."

Ben was half drunk when I got there, but he struggled into his boots and slicker and the three of us made our way to the holler, and then down the steep trail, slipping and sliding through the mud and slush. The waters had backed up until the lower end of the holler was a lake, and we came on Papa standing there, trapped for a way to go any farther. The tracks of the cattle were lost in the water. It looked like they'd waded right into it.

Papa studied for a minute and then he started making his way around the edge, hanging on to limbs and branches. We followed, hard put to keep up on the bank. "The water's risen since they went this way," Papa said, edging onto a rocky ledge, "but if we can get around far enough maybe we'll see them over on the other hill."

Nobody said anything. I don't reckon any of us thought it was likely, but a man has got to do the best he can for his stock. We had to find the cows if we could, and if they were where we could get them out, we had it to do. No kind of a man would heartlessly leave his cattle to drown or starve to death, to say nothing of losing the money they were worth to him.

About halfway around Papa stopped and pointed and we saw them. They were huddled on a little island of dry land that stuck up out of the main current of the creek, but you could tell it wasn't going to be dry very long, for the water was rising fast.

"How'd they get there, Papa?" I asked.

"There's a high spit of land runs out about middle ways," he said, "likely it wasn't flooded yet when they wandered out onto it. They got out there and got caught."

"How long they been broke out?" Faleecy John asked.

Papa shook his head. "It's untelling. Since yesterday . . . or maybe the day before. I was up there to see about them the day before, but they could have broken out right after I was there. From the looks of the water I'd say they've been stranded over there anyways twenty-four hours."

Ben shrugged around and started back up the bank. "Well, they ain't nothin' kin be done fer 'em now, I reckon. Too bad, too. Right smart beef in that herd to lose."

Papa looked at him. "I'm not aiming to lose it if I can help it," he said. "Not without trying, leastways." He turned to me and Faleecy John then. "You boys go get a couple of horses and all the rope you can find."

"What you aimin' to do?" Ben asked.

"Swim over on the horse and drive the cattle back."

"You gone clean crazy, Mark?" Ben shouted. "You cain't git them cows to swim back acrost that channel!"

"I can try."

"Well, mebbe you kin, but I ain't aimin' to git myself drownded tryin' no sich foolishment."

"That's for you to say! You boys go on."

Faleecy John and I climbed back up the holler and

tore over to the barn hard as we could go. Faleecy John saddled a couple of horses and I rolled up all the rope I could find. Wasn't overly much of it, at that, and some pretty old, too. But it would have to do.

We didn't go near the house but Lucibel must have heard the commotion of catching up the horses for she came out on the back porch and yelled at us. "You all find the cows?"

"Yeah," Faleecy John yelled back, "Need the horses to round 'em up."

We swung up on the horses and clipped through the gate. "Ain't no use tellin' her where they're at," he said to me, "hit'd jist weary her."

We were both excited, smelling the danger in what lay ahead and eager to get into it. "Ifen Pa won't try it," Faleecy John said when we kicked the horses down the steep trail into the holler, "I will! I ain't skeered!"

"Me either," I said, talking big. For I was. Scared to death. But I wanted to be in the middle of it just the same.

"Yore pa'll not let you do it," Faleecy John said, "an' hit wouldn't be right fer him to. You're not big enough. I'm almost a man growed."

I knew he was right. I hated not being big enough to do the things Faleecy John did, but at the same time I was filled with admiration for him and proud of him. I knew that if Papa let him ride by his side into that boiling current Faleecy John would do it, and do as well as any man. I didn't doubt it for a minute.

We had to get off and lead the horses the last part of the way. The trail was too steep and slippery, and there was too much chance of sliding into the water. When we got there, Papa and Ben had walked up the bank a piece and had decided on the best place to try, allowing for the current to sweep the horses downstream without missing the island.

Papa took the rope and looked at it, tried different pieces, and then decided on the one that was the longest and strongest looking. He crawled into the saddle. "You coming, Ben?" He looked down at Ben.

Ben looked at the water and then shrugged. "Reckon if a Harbin kin do it, a Squires kin, too."

Faleecy John stepped up then and spoke quick-like, "Pa, let me. I'm might nigh as big as you, an' mebbe stronger. Let me, Pa."

Like a flash of lightning Ben swung on him and knocked him down clean over against a big cottonwood tree. "I said a Squires'd do it," he snarled, and he kicked Faleecy John in the side where he was trying to get up.

Papa was off his horse in a second and had Ben by the coat. "Leave the boy alone," he said, rough and fast, "I've told you before. Leave him alone or I'll kill you!"

Ben was quiet under Papa's hand, and then he spit tobacco juice into a backwash of muddy water. "Let's git it done," he said, and Papa turned him loose.

They crawled on the horses and Papa threw one end of the rope to Ben. "We'd best tie up," he said, "and I'll go first."

When they had each made the rope fast Papa eased the big black out into the water, and it was belly-deep within six foot of the bank. The water there was swirling, but it wasn't fast yet. Papa turned and called back to Ben, "Wait 'til the rope's tight," and he kicked the black on, heading him straight into the current.

In six more feet, just as he nosed into the fast water, the black was swimming. I looked at Ben's horse, and took note that it was a gray, as big and strong-winded as the black. Faleecy John had picked the horses with a good eye. He knew what would be needed in that current.

Ben waited until the rope went taut and then he edged the gray into the water, just a little to the right of where Papa had gone in. It looked awful wide across that stretch of muddy, roiling water, and I knew it was deep, for I knew by the landmarks how far it had backed up the holler. The main current was mighty fast, too. I watched a piece of driftwood race past. It was gone almost by the time I took note of it.

Ben's horse didn't like the water and shied back, but he kicked it hard and it plunged in. What happened then happened so fast I couldn't take it in. One minute the water was boiling around the gray's knees and the next both Ben and the horse were out of sight under the water. I was holding on to a hazelnut bush that leaned out over the water, and it seemed like the bush bent almost double under my weight when they went under. It was Faleecy John leaning against me and holding on. My arm was blue next day where he gripped me. I reckon we both held our breaths. I know we didn't say anything. Didn't anybody. Ben didn't yell, and when the rope jerked Papa looked around, saw what had happened and bent double over it around his waist, but he didn't say anything either.

I reckon just that much difference to the right, and the horse must have stepped off into a deep hole. He came up, floundering and trying to get footing, but Ben was swept off into the fast water. I saw his head once, and an arm hanging on to the rope. I wondered if Papa would be able to stay on the black, or if the black would be pulled downstream too far. The black gave to the rope, but he kept his head and went on swimming. And Papa held on, bent almost double with the rope nigh cutting him in two. We couldn't see Ben, but the rope held tight and as long as it held tight we knew there was a chance of getting him out before he drowned.

The time went slow. · Seemed like the black was standing still with the current churning around him, and all we could see of Papa was his shoulders and head above the water. But when I measured them against the distance to the island I could tell they were making a little headway. I began to breathe a little easier and Faleecy John let go my arm.

Then the rope slacked. One second it was tight and Papa was bending to it. The next, we saw the end of it whip into the air, and then it was gone. That was all.

"The rope broke," I said, and I remembered it was all pretty old. But they'd got so near there! It didn't seem fair for it to hold that far and then break!

Papa turned the black around and headed back toward us. When he got within yelling distance he told us to go for help. "Get Silas," he shouted, "tell him to get half a dozen men with horses! Go on! Don't wait for me. Go on. Quick!"

But it was a week before they found him. Not until the waters had gone down and they could risk a boat on the creek. And then they came up on his body washed up on a gravel beach a mile downstream. It was wedged in with a mass of driftwood, pulpy with water and swollen beyond recognition if they hadn't known who to look for.

Papa was the first to get to him, crawling out of the boat and wading through the drift and the water to his hips. The rope was still tied around Ben's waist, and his hands were gripped tight on it. It was Papa who untied it and loosed his hands from it, and then coiled it up and brought it home. What he did with it we didn't know. We didn't ask, for when he came in with it, he said he never wanted to see it again. Said he felt like he was a murderer.

# sixteen

IT WAS A SHOCK to have Ben go that way, there's no denying. Death in any form is an unwelcome sight. But when a man lays on his own bed and takes leave of the world there's a dignity to it that is fitting to his manhood. In a way he has the comforts of his own kind to the last. It's another thing when a man is swept violently from living to dying right before your eyes. When he is alive, even with all his cussedness, one minute, and gone down fast water, just one arm clutching at life, the next. It leaves you unfeeling and cold, numbed, like you had felt the dying with him. At least that's how I felt for days after Ben was drowned. My hands and feet were cold all the time, and no matter how much I sat before the fire, they wouldn't get warm.

And for all he was only forty-eight at the time, Papa turned old in a week's time. You couldn't put your finger on any one thing to name it, and it wasn't so much the way he looked or the way he acted. Shrunk and drawn into himself, quietened in a corner by the fire, broody and still, his dark skin yellowed and his eyes sunk and hollowed in his head. Everybody said he took it awfully hard and held himself too much to blame. Folks that came all told him nobody could have helped it, not to hold it against himself, that Ben was just meant to go that way. But he'd shake his head and say he hadn't ought to have let Ben try it. That he knew Ben had been drinking and couldn't manage his horse in that current. Ben never was much of a hand with horses anyhow. But nobody faulted him. Everyone knew how hard he had tried to save Ben, for when me and Faleecy John had come back with Silas and the others Papa was riding his horse time and again into the current, trying to find Ben. It was told and retold over the countryside how they'd had to get hold of his horse and hang onto it by main force to stop him. For they knew it was no use, but they couldn't make him listen.

It wasn't until Granny came one day that he got hold of himself. She had no patience with him, it was plain to see. She stood in front of the fire with her back skirts hoisted to warm her legs and all five feet of her was as straight and unbending as a poker. She lipped a mouthful of snuff and wet it down and spit. "Git yer chin up off yer chest, Mark Harbin," she said, "what's done is done! A man does what he has to an' fergits it. Quit actin' like a fool."

Papa looked at her, and I'll swear if it didn't look like some of the straightening from Granny's spine passed over into his. He grinned at her, and it was the first time I'd seen a look of light on his face since it happened. "God, Monnie," he said, "you're tough!"

Granny humphed and spit again. "No use cryin' over spilt milk! They's jist two ways to live, as I see it. One is to be soft an' git licked. The other is to be tough an' do the lickin'. I ain't never been licked."

Papa laughed real soft. "And I ain't aiming to be, Monnie!"

And he chirked up from then on.

All of us felt better then. While Papa was feeling so bad about it, it was like Ben's ghost was riding us. But when he peartened up, we all took fresh heart. It was a fact we soon noticed, too, that things were easier with Ben gone. Faleecy John had been doing the work right along, and he was getting taller and stouter all the time, so it was just natural to expect he could soon be carrying a man's load. There was no talk of anything else and it came to us all that it was a relief not to be worrying about Ben's drinking and beating up on Lydie and Faleecy John, and sulling and slacking on the work. Even Lydie brightened up, and by early summer she'd filled out most of her angles considerably. She told Lucibel it was the hand of the Lord. Said Ben hadn't been doing right for a long time and you couldn't mock God and get by with it forever. He was bound to let you feel his anger soon or late. Lucibel allowed it might be at that. But Granny just snorted and when she went out to the kitchen to get a plate of cookies she was mumbling to herself. "Never seed sich a fool in all my borned days. The hand of the Lord my spavined horse! Reckon she's clean forgot she had ary thing to do with it!"

Papa was as good as his word when my birthday came

around in June and when I woke up that morning there was my gun laying on the bed beside me. Pretty? It was the prettiest sight I ever saw! He'd had a special walnut stock made for it, with my name on a little brass plate sunk in it. Jeff Harbin, it said, and I traced the letters over and over again until my fingers knew the feel of them in the dark.

We put up a target and Faleecy John sighted it in for me. He said it was a beauty. Said it was exactly like his, except for the nameplate. He looked at that and run his fingers over it just like I'd done. "Jeff Harbin," he said out loud.

"Papa could have one put on your gun if you want," I said right quick, thinking his feelings might be hurt. "Likely he just didn't think of it at the time."

Faleecy John sighted down the barrel and his finger squeezed the trigger. Ping! And there was a little round hole right smack in the middle of the ring. He could sure shoot, that boy! He handed me the gun. "All set, now," he said, "you kin shoot a squirrel's eye out an' never run a risk of missin'."

He picked up his own gun that had been leaning up against a tree and eased it into the curve of his arm. He rubbed the grain of the stock and looked down at it. "No," he said, "if yer pa had meant fer mine to have a name on it, he'd of put it there. Think I'll jist leave it be."

Several things stand out in my memory of that year. Come July I started in the eighth grade, my last year in the ridge school. From the first day it was different. I looked at everything with a leave-taking eye, already saying good-bye and storing it up inside to take with me when I went. The old, gray walls that squared in the room. The high windows shafting in the sun. My seat, rubbed shiny by the seat of my pants and those that had gone before me. And the teacher. Even the teacher was the same. That tall, skinny guy that had looked at me the first time I read for him and said, Well, Jeff Harbin! He'd opened a lot of doors for me since then. Taught me a heap. When a country schoolteacher is a good teacher there's none better. Rafe Smollett didn't just go by the books, although he loved them second to nothing. He had a bigness in his mind that went beyond the books. There were no horizons to his thinking, and to those that wanted he held out a spacious and unlimited understanding. I read Shakespeare for the first time that year, and Keats and Milton. And I read Washington Irving and Nathaniel Hawthorne and Walt Whitman. Rafe Smollett's dead, now. Died of the flu in 1918. And I never did rightly thank him for Shakespeare and Walt Whitman. But I reckon he knew. That was his way of saying hail and farewell.

And Jolie let me cut her name and mine inside a heart on an old beech tree by the path one evening. Lord, she was pretty then. She'd cut her hair across her forehead and it lay there in little curls like corkscrews. Made me forever want to reach out and pull them just to see them spring back into place. She was curvey and plump, and her cheeks were as pink as apple blossoms. Her mouth was small and red, and the lips were always moist. I've not forgot the tingle they gave me the first time I kissed them, and the surprise that they clung a little and were warm to touch. For when I'd finished cutting our names and circling the heart around them, she let me kiss her. Once. "Now we're engaged," she said.

At twelve I wasn't very gallant. "How do you mean, engaged?"

"Engaged to be married," she said, "silly! When you kiss somebody it means you're going to be married!"

Golly, my heart pumped a stream of blood up to my head so fast it made me dizzy. At the same time goosebumps of panic prickled down my spine. I didn't know about that! I didn't know whether I wanted to get married or not. I had to swallow three or four times, fast. "Not right away?" I said.

"Oh, for heaven's sake, no! Not 'til we're growed up. Leastways sixteen!"

I felt a tremendous relief. That was a long time yet. Time enough for me to get used to the idea, maybe.

It was not until we'd passed the forks of the trail and she'd turned off that I remembered Faleecy John had kissed her once a couple of years ago. I thought about it as I climbed on up the holler. And I wondered if she was engaged to him, too. That didn't make sense to me, but if you were engaged when you kissed, Faleecy John sure had priority over me!

It was more than my mind could untangle, so I asked Papa about it that night. "Papa, is a woman ever engaged to two men at the same time?"

Papa smoothed his chin and thought about it. "Well, son, I've heard of it, but I wouldn't say it's very common. Why?"

So I told him, and he laughed until he cried. The tears rolled down his cheeks. But Lucibel didn't think it was very funny. She flounced her skirts around her, in a quick whish. "The idea," she said, her nose getting red and her mouth setting straight, "the very idea of that snippet putting such notions in his head!"

Papa and I finally came upon a grain of truth and decided an engagement depended upon who the girl wanted to be engaged to. And we said evidently Jolie didn't want to be engaged to Faleecy John.

# seventeen

T HAT FALL, too, Faleecy John and I started training Snooper to hunt. Faleecy John had a pretty good pack of hounds by now. Five, I think it was. But we started Snooper off just with his mother. A pack will throw a young dog off sometimes, get him excited and flustered in all the confusion. If he starts with his mother or some older dog he learns from the beginning to be steady. No amount of yapping and circling and yelping from the pack will ever confuse him then. He knows his business and he stays with it.

Trixie, Faleecy John's bitch, was as good a fox hound as ever hunted these parts, and after three or four times out with her we could tell Snooper was going to be just as good. Of course he was young and eager, but Trixie held him steady, and he caught on quick.

And then one frosty night, when the moon was old and tired, riding slow across the sky, we tried him with the pack. We went down the ridge toward Hackberry Spur, and we hadn't much more than crossed the holler until the dogs hit a fox trail. They commenced yipping and milling, circling and running out the scent, almost crazy with excitement, their yelps short and sharp, high and broken with eagerness. But it was Trixie and Snooper that snuffed out the track and steadied down to it. Snooper tongued a deep bell note when he hit the trail, clean as a bugle ripping the air. About middle C I'd call that tone, and the sound of it sent a shiver clean down to my heels. I like a hound with a deep voice. Some have a high yelping yip; some start high and steady down low; others have a bass that sounds like a bell. When a pack is milling around, circling, snuffing out the scent, they all sound sharp and separate, like instruments in an orchestra tuning up. But listen to them when the fox is up and they're driving hard! The orchestra is really tuned up then, and you've got the sweetest music in the world! High, low, and in between they sing a master melody, all the parts in harmony. And if you're a fox-hunting man you'll stand and listen and the blood in your veins will run cold with the beauty of it.

That's the way it was that night. The dogs took off down the holler, crossed the branch and were over the hill by the time we'd scrambled down the near side. Their voices sounded far and clear in the night. We breasted the ridge and came out in a thicket of stars that huddled down low in the sky. We stopped and

listened. There was Trixie's high, sharp yip, and
Trigger's steady middle tone. There was Mutt's hoarse,
rough yelp, and deep down below was Snooper's ringing
bell tone. They were circling down below us and they
were hot! Faleecy John got out his old fox horn and
sent a blast over the hill. Lord, it was sweet! Sweet and
sad! The note was blue and low, drawn out and held,
moaning low and melancholy through the air. It
stretched out thin and faint, dying in the distance, and
Faleecy John sent another blast out after it. The dogs
caught the echo and answered it, their voices swelling
back up the hillside exultantly. They were driving
hard, and they were headed back.

"We'd best git over to that old field," Faleecy John
said, "if the fox is headed back he'll likely have to
cross there."

So we made our way down the hill and up to an
abandoned field on the crest of the next hill. It was
rimmed in by old stone walls, most of them fallen in.
But the moon lit up the field enough to give us a shot
if the fox crossed here. We sat down in the shadow to
wait. Nearer and nearer the dogs came. And we hardly
breathed for fear of missing a note. They were back in
the holler now, and suddenly there was a break. You
could tell by the difference in pitch the fox had thrown
them off. Faleecy John let out his breath and it ex-
ploded sharply in the still air. "Lord, if they lose him
now! He's taken to the branch, likely."

But after a moment or two Trixie hit the trail again
and the pack closed in after her. On they came, and we
were shaking with sudden fear. It might be the fox
would keep to the holler and head over the other hill.
He'd pass us by, then, and we'd never see him. The

next minute or two would tell. But the dogs' voices drove steadily up the hill. "Git ready," Faleecy John warned.

A sweat of fear poured out all over me and my skin went clammy and cold. "Is it my shot?" I asked. I hadn't thought but what Faleecy John would take it. I'd never shot a fox. I'd miss, I was certain!

"Hit's yore shot," Faleecy John said, "but wait 'til I speak to him first."

In a cold claw of tremoring I waited and tried to steady down. I kept swallowing, hard and fast. And then we saw a dark shadow race out of the woods and start across the field. That's all he was in the dim light. Just a shadow. Faleecy John nudged me and I got my gun up, but I didn't see how I could possibly hit him. Then Faleecy John called out, "Howdy, Mr. Fox!"

The fox slowed just a little. The strange and unexpected sound threw him off his stride just long enough to make him a good target. I fired and he yelped and leaped high, an then he went down in a long, skidding heap. The next minute the dogs were on him, growling deeply and shaking him.

That speaking to a fox was a trick of Faleecy John's. He'd learned that the sound of the human voice, unusual and unexpected to a fox, would always jar him a little. His reaction would always be to slow a second. Not longer than that, so you had to be ready. But inevitably it threw him off his stride and gave you a good shot.

So I got my first fox. Big? Lord, I felt as tall as the sky! You couldn't have reached me with a ten-foot pole. And when Faleecy John thumped me on the back and said I'd done good I swelled up like a toad. I fairly strutted out to look him over, and when I saw he was a prime red I felt bigger than ever.

There are those that get sentimental and tear-eyed over the killing of animals, crying shame on all hunters. They love to talk of the innocent and harmless game that is wantonly killed by men with guns. But they've not lived in the country and seen their chickens and young lambs carried off by foxes, or watched their young fruit trees stripped of buds by gray squirrels. Game may be innocent, but it's a far cry from being harmless most times. And we didn't kill wantonly. We killed squirrels and rabbits for eating, and there's no better eating in the world. And we killed foxes because they were thieving varmints. But there was no law that said we needn't enjoy the hunting at the same time. I'd be the first to admit that there never was a ridge man yet didn't love to hunt. I'd say the three things a ridge man loves most to do are first, to hunt . . . second, to burn off a field high with broom sedge . . . and third, to make love. In that order, I'd swear it!

We hunted foxes to keep them killed off so as to protect our property, but there was another reason, too. A good gray pelt brought from five to ten dollars those days, and a prime red one was worth twenty dollars. And Faleecy John made a right smart money on the side that way.

He was doing what he'd said he would the day they moved in the rent house. He was buying Lydie things to take the place of their old house plunder. He'd got her a kitchen range that was as nice as Lucibel's. A big Pearl Blue Ribbon, with a water reservoir that held fifteen gallons, and with a roomy, porcelain-front warming closet up above. Lydie was really proud of it. He was saving now for a dresser. He knew exactly the kind he wanted. Nice, shiny oak with a good mirror in a frame. And he wanted rugs on the floors. Said he wasn't going to be satisfied until they had linoleums all over, and a real carpet in the fireplace room. Seemed like he set a heap of store by those rugs. All along he was laying back a little, too, to buy some land with. He'd not forgot he aimed to quit renting some day.

So he hunted foxes with more reason than most. We hunted at night for the joy of it, and I don't know but that we both liked it best. But Faleecy John got more foxes early of a morning. Saturday was the only day we could hunt in the morning, for he had work to do the other days, and I had to go to school. But nearly every Saturday morning we got up before first light and set out. It was one of those Saturday mornings Faleecy John had words with Carney Turner, Jolie's pa.

On the ridge it's an unwritten law not to kill another man's fox, once he's got him up. You don't do it, that's all. I've known men to cease speaking for life over such a thing, and the feuding between the Nicholses and the Jordans over on Tommyhawk Ridge begun over Bud Jordan shooting Jim Nichols' fox. Bud wouldn't back down, so Jim plugged him right between the eyes. There was bad blood and killing amongst them for ten years. So you will understand why Faleecy John had words with Carney Turner.

We'd got an early start that morning and had followed the dogs down into Little Lost Creek valley. Faleecy John figured the fox's circuit would bring him back around onto the hillside past Carney Turner's place, so we took our stand in a clearing there we thought likely the fox would use for a crossing.

We figured right and the dogs were driving hard, not so very near, but we could hear them plain, when the fox trotted out into the clearing. He knew he had plenty of time so he wasn't in any hurry. Looked like he knew he had them fooled and was just enjoying himself. He even stopped to lick at a paw, and Faleecy John had his gun up in a second. Before he could fire, though, a shot rang out across the clearing and the fox dropped.

Faleecy John let his gun down and he stood there a second, too startled to think. Then the blood rushed to his face and he started cussing so fast he choked on his own cuss-words. He took out across that clearing like the devil was on his heels. "Goddammit to hell!" he yelled, "that was my fox! What business you got shootin' a man's fox, anyways! Cain't you hear them hounds? Come on out of them woods, an' I'll learn you to kill a man's fox!"

It was Carney Turner came out of the woods and moved slowly toward Faleecy John. He had a mouthful of tobacco juice and he shot a stream sideways out the corner of his mouth. He didn't appear to be ruffled at all. "Howdy," he said, and he walked on over toward the fox. Faleecy John had pulled up short and he walked towards the fox, too. But I could tell from the way he was breathing he was still as mad as a hornet.

"Never heared yore dogs," Turner said, looking down at the fox. He had a funny high-pitched voice that came out through his nose. Always rubbed me the wrong way. I didn't see how he could help hearing the dogs, and I reckon that's what Faleecy John thought, too.

"We could hear 'em plain as day," he said, and I knew from the thick roughness in his throat he was barely holding on to himself.

"You was listenin' fer 'em," Turner said, "you doubtin' my word?" and he sliced a look across the fox at Faleecy John.

Faleecy John eyed him, and he toed the dead fox. "Not if I git the pelt," he finally said, and I chuckled inside. That was putting it right up to Carney Turner.

Turner showed a deep red. "That's jist the same as callin' me a liar," he said.

But it wasn't. If he'd actually killed the fox not hearing the dogs he'd be willing for Faleecy John to have the pelt. That would be only right. It would be in the nature of apologizing. So when he made that answer it was plain as day he'd deliberately killed the fox, knowing it belonged to somebody else, and not caring. I hadn't thought he was that kind of man, and it sickened me a little.

"You named it," Faleecy John said, and his voice was so flat and dry you could tell he was calling Carney's hand.

"Cain't nobody call me a liar an' git by with it," Turner said thickly.

"Hit's jist up to you," and Faleecy John spraddled his legs a little and I noticed he was holding his gun easy and loose, so's he could drop it quick if Turner made a move.

Faleecy John was just fifteen, but for all that he was nearly six foot tall, broad and thick through the shoulders, and his hands were twice as big as any other man's. He stood tight and ready, and he towered a good six inches over Turner. I reckon Turner took all that in as he studied, and I reckon he decided he didn't want anything Faleecy John could give him, for he turned away finally. Shouldered his gun and walked off. "Hell," he said, "you're jist a kid! I ain't aimin' to fight no kid. You kin have the pelt. But I'll not fergit this day. Don't think I will. We'll have a settlin' when yer growed up!"

Faleecy John bounced like a cock rooster sharpening his spurs. "I'm growed up enough right now to settle ary thing you've got to settle, Carney Turner. C'mon back here an' have it out."

But Turner kept going.

We watched him disappear into the woods, and then we set to skinning the fox. It was a prime red one, and ordinarily Faleecy John would have been crowing with pleasure. But he was scowly and black-faced, quiet and in-turned while we worked. "Reckon I've made me an enemy," he said finally. "Reckon he'll allus be set agin me, now."

"But you couldn't help it, Faleecy John," I said. "You couldn't have done any different, seeing it was your fox."

He shrugged. "I know that. That's why I done it. You've got to take yer own part."

"He surely heard the dogs," I insisted, "they were pretty far off, but we could hear them plain."

"Shore he heard 'em. But even if he hadn't of, he would of wanted to do what was right, if he'd been on the level. He was wantin' the pelt!"

And that was the first we knew that the Turners were having a bad time. When we told Papa he pondered it a minute and allowed Carney likely was having trouble meeting his notes at the bank. "He's not a very managing man," Papa said, "and I heard last summer he'd had to put a mortgage on his place."

"Well, if I'd of knowed he needed the money from the pelt . . ." Faleecy John started to say.

But Papa warned him off. "No," he said, "you did

right. Even if Carney's needing money he's got no call to go killing another man's fox. We can't have a man doing that kind of thing here on the ridge and getting by with it. Carney'll have to get his money the right way."

And that was all was said about it.

# eighteen

T HE NEXT three years I wasn't on the ridge much, for I went away to school the fall after I was thirteen in the summer. I went to the same school Papa had gone to when he was a boy, for he'd liked it and he held that a parochial school was better for a boy away from home than a public school. Maybe it was at that. There's something to say for having a youngster under the care of his teachers twenty-four hours a day. It makes his whole life a school, and there's more to learning than what goes on in the classroom.

The school was at Merrittville, just twenty miles from home, and of course I went back when I could. But it wasn't as often as you'd expect, being so close.

We didn't have many holidays and we didn't get the whole summer like kids that went to public school. St. Luke's had its own farm and dairy and all of us had work to do outside of classes. The spring and summer were heavy seasons on the farms. But I went home for Easter and Christmas, and for the month of August each year I was there.

I liked it there. I was homesick for the ridge, and I never did get to where I didn't think about it a lot and look toward the day when I'd be going home to stay. But by and large I liked it. The priests were scholars and good teachers, and the school had one of the largest libraries in the state. It was a pleasure to have the use of it. They were also good farmers, up-to-date and modern, with good equipment. Knowing I was to have the running of the farm some day Papa had told them I was especially to learn agriculture, although he didn't want anything else neglected.

So I got a good, well-rounded education. The classics, history, government, economy, agriculture. I don't know of anything else that better fits a man for living. To study man and his history, and to study the soil and its production. That goes a long way to fit a man for understanding life itself. It was better than a high-school education, without being as advanced as college. Taken all the way around, it was mighty good.

I missed Faleecy John, though. And wished he could have come with me. He would have come, too, if he could have. For all he hadn't liked the ridge school, seemed like he realized what he'd be missing. Just a few nights before I left he was at our house for supper. And all of us were talking in a big way about me going. "I'd shore like to be goin', too," Faleecy John said, "an education is a powerful help to a body," and he looked across the table at Papa. "Yores has helped you a heap, ain't it, Mr. Harbin?"

Papa laid down his fork and took a swallow of coffee. "Well, yes, Yes, of course. But a man can be a good farmer without it, Faleecy John, if he's quick to learn the best ways of farming, and takes advantage of things that come his way."

"That's what I meant," Faleecy John said quickly. "Hit learns you the things to take advantage of."

Papa looked at him slow-like and his face went still. Then he picked up his fork and went on eating. Faleecy John bent over his plate which Lucibel had helped with more chicken and dumplings. But he looked up again in a minute, like he had just thought of something. "Ain't it funny the difference hit makes who yer pa an' ma is?"

I'd thought the same thing so many times that it sounded strange, coming from him. I'd never talked about it with him, but it was like he was speaking my own thoughts. I couldn't never take credit for being me, Jeff Harbin. It was because my papa was Mark Harbin, and my mother was Lucibel. And I'd often thought how terrible it would be to have it different, and had felt sorry for Faleecy John on account of Ben and Lydie. Now, because I was Jeff Harbin I was going away to school. And because he was Faleecy John Squires, Faleecy John couldn't go. And it didn't anyways seem right and fair.

Papa shoved his chair back and stood up. Lucibel looked at him. "You're not through, Mark? There's custard pie."

But Papa said he didn't want any and he went on to the other room. And before we'd finished our pie he went out to the barn. Didn't come in until after

Faleecy John had gone home. I thought maybe he was feeling bad about Faleecy John, like I was. But he'd done as much as could be expected for somebody not even kin to him.

"I reckon Papa's not feeling very good," Lucibel said, when she started stacking up the dishes.

"I reckon not," Faleecy John agreed. And then he laughed. "Lucibel, me an' Jeffie'll do the dishes. You go on in an' play on the organ. We kin hear from here."

Like everything else he did, Faleecy John was good at a woman's work when he turned his hand to it. He washed and I dried, and you couldn't of told but Lucibel had done it herself. We left the kitchen spotless, with fresh water drawn for morning, and the woodbox piled high for the breakfast fire. We sang a little with Lucibel, after, and then Faleecy John went home.

Yes, I missed him. Missed him a lot. And I wrote to him pretty often, without hearing much from him back. He wasn't any hand to write. But Lucibel wrote about him. She wrote regular every week, long letters that went just like she talked, gay and happy-like. It was just like having a visit at home when I'd get a letter. She told all the things she knew I wanted to hear. Like the brindle cow losing her calf, and the first hay cutting being extra heavy, and how she'd painted the kitchen, and guess what color? I laughed at that, and didn't have to guess but once. I knew she'd painted it yellow. She'd have painted the whole house yellow if Papa would of let her, I reckon. She loved it so good.

And she'd tell about Faleecy John. How he'd finally got the linoleums for the house and the carpet for the fireplace room. "Looks real pretty," she said. "He got a pattern all over roses with bright green leaves, and it cheers up the room a heap." She told, too, how he'd bought a couple of heifers from Papa and was aiming

to start him a dairy herd. And how Papa was letting
him work a little tobacco patch of his own down close
to the big field so's he could get in a lick at it handy
when he'd be through with Papa's. And she mentioned
that Faleecy John was talking to Jenny Clark a right
smart. She didn't seem to think much of the idea, but
it didn't surprise me any. Lucibel said she *did* hope
Faleecy John had better sense than to tie himself up to
the girl. But as far as I coud remember Jenny Clark
had always been counted a smart girl, handy to work
and stout, and would of made a good wife for most any
fellow. I didn't like the idea of Faleecy John getting
married at all. But I wasn't going to worry about it
being Jenny Clark. For I didn't think he'd be trying
to set himself up housekeeping with any girl until he
had that little piece of land he'd always talked about. I
made sure he'd get that safe, first. I figured I knew
what he was talking to Jenny Clark for, too. But that
was something I couldn't tell Lucibel.

When I'd go home everything was just the same.
We'd hunt or fish or swim, and of course, work. On
Sundays we would saddle up and go to a singing or a
preaching somewheres, and our girls would be there
and it would be pretty fine. My girl was still Jolie
Turner, and she got prettier every year. Faleecy John,
mostly, would be with Jenny, but sometimes he
wouldn't. Sometimes Ida Stone would be with us, but
you couldn't say she would pair off with Faleecy John.
It would just be the four of us all together when she
was along. I was always glad when Ida would be with
us. For then it was different. We'd just have fun riding
and racing the horses, or spreading a dinner the girls
had brought, all of us laughing and hungry and joking
with one another.

When Jenny was with us her and Faleecy John would

always go off by theirselves at one time or another. It always made me have a funny feeling, and I was afraid Jolie would catch on. I didn't see how she could help, for they were never too careful around us. Always hugging and kissing in front of us, like we wasn't there. And Faleecy John would kid us and make like we must be made of stone or something. I hugged and kissed Jolie . . . some. But not in public. I never held her light that way. And I told Faleecy John so. "Jolie and I are going to get married some day," I told him. "There's time enough for all that then."

I remember how he threw his head back and laughed. He made the hills ring with echoes. "It's too good to waste, Jeffie," he said. "You better take it while you kin git it."

But I didn't. I didn't want it that way.

Then the last year I was in school Lucibel's letters weren't so gay. Papa was ailing, she said, and he was some worried about Faleecy John. Not that Faleecy John was slacking off the work, she went on to say, but he was deviling Papa to sell him a piece of land, and Papa couldn't see his way to do it. The piece Faleecy John wanted was part of the best land, although we'd never cleared it. It laid level and I knew Papa meant to clear it and work it as soon as I got home. With so much of the ridge hills and hollers, it takes a pretty big farm to have enough level land to do much good. We'd never thought we had an acre to spare, and Faleecy John must of known that. Lucibel said she reckoned Faleecy John was so used to living near and working our land he couldn't hardly think of buying off somewheres. Anyway, he'd spoken of this piece of Papa's and wouldn't hardly take no for an answer. Lucibel said she'd be powerfully glad when I was through school and could come home to stay, for Papa needed me bad.

She mentioned, too, that Jenny Clark had got married. Married a fellow from over at Persimmon Ridge. Which surprised me a little. I'd not heard of her ever talking to anybody but Faleecy John. But I had the answer when I got a letter from Faleecy John himself a day or two later. One of the few I ever got from him. He said he reckoned I'd heard Jenny was married. Said it was just in time, too. She was five months gone. Said she'd cried and taken on terrible trying to get him to marry her, but he wasn't ready to get married yet, and when he did it wouldn't be Jenny Clark. But he'd felt sorry for her and had talked this fellow over at Persimmon Ridge into going with her a time or two, and by priming him with a few drinks had finally got him in the notion of marrying her. So that was a worry off his hands. And her being married wouldn't make no difference if he ever wanted to be with her again.

I could see his black eyes scheming the whole thing out, and hear him chuckling when he pulled it off! There was a cold-bloodedness about Faleecy John that chilled you clean to the bones, times. He took what he wanted, and he'd pay just what he wanted to pay. He'd had Jenny for years, when he wanted her. But he never did intend to marry her. I didn't know, then, what his plans were, but I could have told Jenny from the start they didn't include her. He wasn't going to waste anything that came his way. But he wasn't going to let anything or anybody swerve him from what he'd set his heart on.

Sometimes, like when I had read that letter, I thought I didn't ever want any more of Faleecy John. He could be so brutal and he was always so lustful.

But then I'd remember all the good things about him,
and how, always, with me he'd been fine. Patient, careful, and understanding. And he wasn't so different at
that from most of the men on the ridge. You'd have
to know a ridge man to know how I mean that. Not that
they're callous of deep emotions and feelings, or that
they don't hold love to be good and right. They do.
There's not much divorce on the ridge. A man marries
his girl and they make out a life together. But that
don't keep him from taking what he can get from anybody else, either before or after the wedding. There's
no question of morals to it. A man don't think
whether it's right or wrong. It's as simple as eating
when you're hungry, or sleeping when you're tired. If
a woman's willing, you go to bed with her, and it's
forgotten as quick as it's over. It don't mean a man
loves his wife a bit less. And he don't feel like he's been
particularly unfaithful. He's just done what comes
natural to his appetites. But you don't catch many
ridge men having what's nowadays called an affair with
a woman. He's got his wife for regular and steady.
What would he want with another one? That's what
he'd call being unfaithful.

None of this means he flaunts it in the face of his
wife. Lord, no. He sure wouldn't want her to know,
for it would go against the grain of any woman to
know such. He takes care that she don't know. But
that's not because he's ashamed of it. It's mostly for her
peace of mind.

And he sure wouldn't want her doing the same thing
as him. He'd be the laughingstock of the ridge if he'd
put up with such a thing. It's the strictest double
standard you ever saw. I'm not excusing it, and I
never followed it. But that's the way it is, mostly, and

for all it looked like Faleecy John was so callous, I knew he wasn't doing much more than any other man on the ridge would of done. Hardly any man would of married a girl he could have without. But for him to scheme to get her married off safe. That was Faleecy John. Most would of waited it out. Until the girl's pa either come with a shotgun or the law. Or the girl had her youngun and raised it alone. But Faleecy John felt sorry for her, at the same time he wouldn't do a thing for her himself, and saw to it she was taken care of. Saw to it at the same time he could go back if he wanted to.

I had to laugh. What a warped sense of justice he had!

When I went home to stay I was pushing sixteen and Faleecy John was eighteen and a half. Men grown, we were. Every time I had gone home Papa had looked older and more careworn. His face had got lined and his eyes were sunk and he'd thinned down considerable. He wouldn't own up to feeling bad, but it was plain to be seen he wasn't like he used to be. He couldn't do the work he used to could, either. It was time me and Faleecy John took over.

But I wanted to get the straight about this piece of land Faleecy John wanted. So I asked Papa straight out.

"I reckon I'll let him have it," Papa said. We were sitting in the front yard under the big maple tree, and the afternoon sun sheened his black hair which wasn't even yet turning gray. "It's that piece that joins on to the lower pasture. Never been cleared yet. I've been saving it against the day you'd be home. It's nice and level and will make good tobacco ground. It's not as if I'd made much use of it. It's a right pretty piece of land, though, and I thought you'd need it some day."

He rubbed his hand over his eyes like he did so much of the time nowadays. Like he was worn out with seeing things too clear, or maybe not clear enough. I don't know. But he never used to have restless habits like that and it bothered me a heap. Seemed like he was trying to brush something away. "By and large Faleecy John has been mighty good to help all these years," he went on, "and I've encouraged him to save to buy his own land. I've helped him every way I could. But it didn't occur to me he'd be wanting to buy from me. I thought he'd rather get out on his own some place. He's taken a fancy to that piece, though, and claims he don't want any other. Says he don't want an old, worked-out farm. He wants new ground, and he wants to build his own house. I don't rightly know how I'd have got along without him these past years, with you gone to school and all. And I feel a right smart obligated to him."

"You're willing to let him have it, then?" I asked.

He rubbed his hand across his eyes again. "Well, yes. I reckon so. If you are, that is. I've not told him yes or no. At least not lately. I gave him a flat no when he first named it. But he's brought it up two or three times since, and finally I said I'd think more of it. But the place will come to you some day," and his eyes went past me to the rim of our land flattened against the crest of the ridge and his voice got soft, "likely not so distant in time, either," and then he pulled his eyes back and laughed. "Well, anyway. What I'm trying to say is that if you want to hold all of it I'll tell Faleecy John he can't have the piece. I'm not going to split your inheritance for you, no matter what." There was vigor in that last statement and fire in his eyes. Like he'd been pushed too far and had stood, finally.

"Lord, Papa," I said, "the place'll be big enough for me without that thirty acres! If we're obligated to Faleecy John, and doubtless we are, for I've thought myself he's done more than just a renter would have done for us, and in a way his place with us has always been more like he was kin to us." Papa's hand went to his eyes again, but I went on, "If we're obligated in any way, I'd want to see us pay it in full. But more than that, you know it would please me a heap to have him settled close by. There's nothing I'd like better, so if that piece of land is what Faleecy John wants, and if it's me you're thinking of in trying to decide, don't give it another thought. There's plenty for me."

Papa let his hand drop and I noticed how thin it had got, and how big the veins stood up on the back. And the brown liver spots. Like an old man's hands, I couldn't help thinking. It hurt me to look at them. I couldn't stand to have Papa getting old. I'd not thought a lot about it before. Him being thirty-six when I was born. But now it struck me I wasn't going to have a lot of time to be with him, and to work by his side taking a man's part. He was getting too old now, and I was just shooting up to full growth. There was a sadness in the whole thought.

Then Papa smiled at me and his face was lighted with sweetness. "You're a fine boy, Jeff," he said. They'd left off calling me Jeffie when I went away to school. "A fine boy. I'm mighty proud of you." And then there was quiet again before he went on. Like he was thinking what he had to say next. "Jeff . . . there's one thing I'd like you to remember. Remember it always. You and Lucibel have been the heart and core of my life. Whatever mistakes I've made, Jeff . . . and I've made them, had nothing to do with you or Lucibel. Don't forget that."

I was puzzled, for I didn't know of a wrong thing Papa had ever done in his life. But thinking to humor him I said, "Why, of course, Papa. We know that. Lucibel and me. We'll always know that."

And then we went in the house, for Lucibel was calling us to supper.

# nineteen

I RECKON Faleecy John was about the happiest boy in
kingdom come when Papa told him he was going to
let him have the land. He was so full of it he was pranc-
ing! Papa told him they'd close the deal the next spring
when Faleecy John had all the money. He never
offered to take less than the land was worth, on account
of it being Faleecy John wanting it. He just named a
price that was right, and Faleecy John said it was fair
enough. He lacked a couple of hundred dollars having
it. But come spring he'd have it. After the winter's
trapping. So all of us counted it as good as done.

That next Saturday night we rode over to Persimmon
Ridge. Nearly all the young bucks close around would
gather over there on Saturday nights. Enos Higgins

and his boy, Walt, had a still somewheres near Lo and Behold and they'd bring down a batch of moonshine to the old log school in the holler and those that wanted could buy and drink.

This county was dry, even in those days, and stilling was clearly against the law. But nobody bothered much about that. Ridge folks have always had their own idea of abiding by the law, and while there were plenty that didn't hold with stilling and drinking, they wouldn't of thought of turning Enos in.

That was my first Saturday night with that crowd, and it was an eye-opener, all right. They were pretty good boys, mostly, but Saturday night was their night to hell a little. They built up a fire down in the woods a piece from the schoolhouse and set around talking and laughing and drinking. The talk was pretty rough. Mostly about women. Ones they'd had, and ones they'd like to have, and a lot of bragging and shooting the bull. One fellow said he was keeping count of the different ones and he'd had ten, and he was twenty years old. He acted like he thought that was pretty good. Faleecy John ripped out a snort and asked him what he'd been doing in his spare time. Said he kept count, too, and he'd had eighteen! A different one for every year he was old. The whole crowd roared at him, but you could tell they wouldn't of put it past him.

"Jist goin' to add one a year, Faleecy John?" Ab Barnes wanted to know. Ab was a short, roly-poly little feller, good-natured as the day is long and always ready to make a joke.

"Naw," Faleecy John said "I'm figgerin' on doublin' it when I git to be a man!"

That's the kind of talk they made. Some of it. Some was good, plain man talk, and if you weren't too squeamish you counted it all good, plain man talk. They were boys that knew one another since childhood, knew what to take for truth and what to discount for bragging. It was a part of being a ridge boy and becoming a ridge man. Like the initiation rites in some of those primitive tribes you read about. It was a testing and a mettling. Maybe it was coarse and crude. I guess it was, in a way. I reckon they done and said things would hackle the hairs on a fastidious parson's neck. But if you stop and think about it long enough, sex is not very fastidious anyways. At least I wouldn't think it would be very good if it was. Any way you look at it, it's sex. You can dress it up and call it beautiful and spiritual and all the words these marriage experts nowadays like to tag onto it. Between a man and woman that's made a good marriage there's all of those things. But they don't depend necessarily on sex. They're there, all through the whole of living together. But you refine sex too much and you've not got anything left. Get it too spiritual and it goes away. It ought always to be the male and the female . . . like they were made to be. Lusty and strong and fine. Not that what these men said was like that always. But it was a part of it. It was at least the knowing what sex was meant to be.

I took my first drink of moonshine that night and set and held my stomach for an hour. I thought I was on fire! Faleecy John and the rest of them laughed until they rolled in the leaves. But Lord have mercy! It was the closest thing to man-made lightning I ever saw. I watched Faleecy John match drink for drink with every man there, and I didn't see how he got it down in the first place, nor held it there once it was down, in the second! But it looked like he could drink a barrelful and never show it except to laugh and sing a little louder.

Along about midnight we got on our horses and rode hell for leather down the ridge shooting off our guns. Made a whale of a racket and waked up the whole countryside. But we were too full of oats to ride home peaceable. You know how it is. A young man, prime and full of juice, a high moon and a crisp night, a strong horse between your legs! Man, you've just got to shoot all six of them cartridges!

We went over nearly every Saturday night after that. Lucibel was some worried about it, for everybody knew what went on those nights. But Papa just laughed and said leave us be. He'd done the same in his day, and I reckon he knew it wouldn't do a good man any harm, and if one was naturally bad it wouldn't be the company had made him so.

But there did some things happen that winter oughtn't to of happened, and they ended with a killing. But you couldn't blame that on the Saturday nights, or the drinking, or even the pranking. It was just one man's meanness. Sim Parker told you about that. If I remember right Sim told you about it and you wrote it up and had it printed in one of those magazines in the east.

It was Walt Higgins caused it all. You'll recollect there was four boys had growed up good friends there on Persimmon Ridge. Walt Higgins, Sim Parker, Silas Tucker and Ab Barnes. And how Silas and Ab took a liking for the same girl, Liza Simmons. And you'll remember Walt was sneaking enough to play one against the other until he had them so they wouldn't hardly speak to one another.

Me and Faleecy John were with the bunch the night they burned old man Simmons' haystacks, and we remembered it was Walt thought it up, although Ab got the blame for it. And it made old man Simmons so mad he forbid Ab ever to come see Liza again. And then when Zeb Barnes' coon hounds were high-lifed, we were there, and we knew who'd thought of that, too. But he managed to get Silas blamed for that. Like he was taking revenge on Ab, for Zeb was Ab's pa.

But we weren't there the night Ab was knifed to death. I had a cold that night and we didn't go to Persimmon Ridge. So we couldn't rightly say what had happened. But it sobered everybody up considerable when the law took Silas for it, and finally penitentiaried him. He'd claimed to have left the crowd when they started down the ridge, but they found his mule with bloodtsains on the blanket the next morning tied in a grove back of the church where Ab's body was left.

Sim told you how Silas died the first year of his sentence and how Walt and Liza got married. And then how when he was made sheriff he run it down and learned it was Walt had done the whole thing, just to get Liza. You'll recollect that Walt was convicted and executed for the murder, two murders you might say, and then bless patty, if Sim Parker didn't up and marry Liza himself!

The whole thing made quite a stir. But Faleecy John said right from the start it was Walt had done it. He didn't have any proof. Just his knowledge of Walt and the others. He said it was just the damfool, stupid kind of thing Walt would do. "Now if *I* wanted somebody else's girl," he said, "I'd never do murder to get her. There's a hell of a lot easier way to work it than that!"

"What would you do?" I said.

"Why, I'd git some sort of hold on him, an' jist commence squeezin'. Hit wouldn't be necessary to kill a man at all. Jist squeeze him until he let go, is the way I'd do it."

I've thought of that many's the time, since.

# twenty

**B**UT OF COURSE all that took time happening, and has got nothing to do with this story anyhow. I just recalled it in connection with what Faleecy John said. There was still the summer and fall ahead when I got home.

When I walked over the place the next morning I thought it had never looked so pretty and fine before. The pastures were green and lush and the cattle looked fat and solid. The tobacco was just beginning to turn and the sun slanted pure gold off the broad, yellowing leaves. It was going to be a prime crop. When I walked down the trail through the holler to Little Lost Creek the woods closed over me cool and green and quiet, and I felt filled up and running over with contentment. The creek ran shallow and clear over the sands, and in dark pools the sides of sun fish glinted like swift-speeding rainbows.

It was a good time to be coming home. It had always been good to get home from school, but this time it was different. This time it belonged to me . . . forever and enduring it was mine. And that made a world of difference. That was what made it look so pretty and so fine. It was all mine, now. I was never to lose another minute of it, and it was like I swelled to take it all in. The pastures and the cattle, the home place so solid and so stout, the woods and the hollers and the creek. In a new way they were part of me, not ever to be lost again.

And it was fine to be with the people that were mine. Papa, for all he was changing, was still Papa. Tall, dark, straight, the fine edges of time cutting small lines in his face and veining his hands, but leaving him still the humor, the judgment, the pride of Mark Harbin. It came over me again how good it was to be his son. What a fine thing it was to be Jeff Harbin.

Lucibel had changed little. She was thirty-two now. Mighty young to be having a grown, strapping son. Her hair had darkened some. It wasn't quite the pure yellow it had been in first youth. But it was still bright and glowing, and the face beneath it showed no sign of the years. Most ridge women age early, losing their teeth and sagging their shoulders. But Lucibel had been more protected than most from the dragging, heavy burdens of work, and she had always had such a pride in herself that she kept her shoulders up and her waist trim and neat. She was now as slim and quick and full of life as I could ever remember her. And that first evening I was home I sat in the kitchen with Papa and watched her flash from the stove to the table setting out supper, her laugh coming and going in her pleasure that I was home, her yellow dress starched and rustly with her movements, and I thought for the thousandth time how wonderful she was, how different, how sweet and clean and good. Oh, I knew what blessings were mine, and I counted them over and over the next few days.

And maybe, in my heart, the best of all was Faleecy John. Whatever I felt for Lucibel and Papa was good. But Faleecy John was the other part of myself, and it was like being whole again to saddle up and ride down the ridge road again with him, knowing that life stretched out ahead of us with no more separations and no more interruptions. I could draw a deep breath, now, and look down the years ahead. Faleecy John was going to be no farther away than the piece of timbered land Papa was letting him buy. All my life I could look across the pastures and see his place and know he was there. It was the last thing to fill my cup to overflowing.

Once Papa had made up his mind to let Faleecy John have the land he acted as pleased as the rest of us to see him finally reaching what he'd set for himself. We'd known for so long what he wanted, and had watched him work hard for it. Couldn't nobody fault Faleecy John that way, then. He'd never dodged a piece of work in his life. And his aim to have land of his own was a good one that made us all proud of him.

Of course in time it meant that Papa would have to get new renters, but he never was one to stand in the way of a man bettering himself. He'd helped Silas Clark get his start, and others before him, and with Faleecy John so much like part of the family he'd helped him more than anyone else.

So he listened to Faleecy John's talk of what he wanted to do, and gave advice when he was asked for it. And I felt proud that both of them asked what I thought sometimes, on account of me learning some new ideas over at St. Luke's. Faleecy John already had the start of a few dairy cows, and he meant to build them up. He figured there was good money to be made in dairy farming.

Him and me would go over there and look at the piece and he'd talk about what he aimed to do. Clear it, first off, and use the timber to make lumber for the house. "There'll be a plenty," he said, "fer house an' barns, too. Good, stout oak. I'll put the house on that knoll over there, an' leave enough trees around it fer shade. I want me four rooms down, an' two up. Sided an' painted, too. Like your'n. This ain't goin' to be no shack jist throwed up any old way. I want me a purty place."

It was a nice piece of land, lying level to rolling, and when he'd talk I could see it taking shape. He paced off the house and yard and the garden patch. And then he laid out the barns. "I'll put the tobacco in that field yon side the barn," he said, "on the south slope, so's it'll git the sun. An' the corn an' pastures out back. Oh, hit'll be nice when I git through," he promised.

He was jubilant those days in the fall, prancy and full of juice. He couldn't talk of anything but his place, and it got so that was about all any of us thought of. And it pleased us all mighty fine.

It was Papa suggested he go on and build one of his barns before cold weather. We'd got the work caught up on the place, short of stripping the tobacco, which we couldn't do until it had cured anyhow. And Papa said there'd be time for me and Faleecy John to fell and drag up the logs for the barn before we'd be needed again. And when we got them all dragged up we could have a barn-raising and Faleecy John would have him a good, tight barn for his cows that winter.

That suited us fine and all through the clear, crisp days of late September and the whole month of October we were in the timber over on Faleecy John's place, marking and felling trees. It takes a sight of logs to build a sizeable barn, but the work went fast under our hands. A happy worker makes a quick job, I've noticed. And first thing we knew we had enough logs down and it was time to start snaking them to the building site.

Carney Turner came by one day. We were eating the lunch Lucibel had put up for us and he sat down on the end of the log and passed the time of day. "Mr. Harbin building him another barn?" he asked.

"Naw. This un's mine," Faleecy John said.

"Your'n!"

"Yeah. I'm buyin' this piece offen him. Jist commenced clearin' it the other day. Goin' to build hereabouts come spring. Thought I'd git one of the barns up before winter sets in."

Carney rubbed his chin and pondered the news. "Well, now," he said finally, "that's fine, ain't it? You're kinder comin' up in the world, Faleecy John."

"I allus aimed to own me a piece of land some day. Never did aim to stay a renter fer long. I've got me a start of milk cows, too," Faleecy John bragged, "an' before long I'll be makin' 'em pay me good money!"

Carney nodded and stood up. "Allus did like to see a ambitious young feller. I hope you do good, Faleecy John. I shore do."

He went off through the woods and we watched him go. Faleecy John ate the last of a piece of cake and dusted his hands against the side of his pants. "Talked too much then," he said, "ort not to of. He's still havin' a hard time makin' out, an' it went too much like braggin' to speak of it in front of him."

"I don't know," I said, "it'll be all over the ridge when we get these logs ready for the raising. There's not many don't know already you're buying the place."

Faleecy John stood up and stretched. The sun was bright on his head and I noticed again how black and shiny his hair was. The same crow's wing black of Papa's. He was pushing nineteen, now, and had his full growth. Six feet four, he stood, and his span from finger tip to finger tip was nigh six foot six. He wedged down from those broad shoulders into a lean waist as flat as a pancake, and his flanks were as slim as a coon hound's. He was as handsome a man as ever walked this ridge. He was that.

"Well," he said, yawning, "what's one man's meat is another one's poison, I reckon. Carney had him a nice little place an' couldn't manage right. I'm sorry fer that. But it ain't nothin' off my back. I got my own way to make, an' I got no time to waste."

It was just past the first of November when we sent the word around of the barn-raising. We hoped for a clear, fair day. And it was. Frosty and nippy, but not too cold. Just the right kind of day for the kind of work we aimed to do. The men'd work up a good sweat in the sun, without chilling off in a cold wind that so often blows that time of year. It looked like the weather had just been made special for the barn raising.

If you've never been to a barn-raising you don't know how good it is. On the ridge here there's not many social events. Folks mostly go about the business of living pretty serious. Church once a month when the preacher comes, an all-day singing ever' month or two somewheres round about, a sociable over at the school occasionally, and that's about the extent of it. Other wise folks depend on taking dinner with one another on Sundays, and the common give and take of passing the road.

So a barn-raising was quite an affair . . . a social event, and all would come from miles around. The men would come to help raise the barn, and the women folks would bring food and cook it there on the grounds, and the children would run around getting in the way generally, but having a mighty fine time doing it. Somebody would likely bring a fiddle, and somebody else would throw in his old banjo or guitar at the last minute, and when the barn was raised there'd be music and some frolicking. There'd be a jug hidden off down in a thicket, too, and from time to time a couple of the men would slip off down there and take a swig. Not enough to make them walk the ridgepole unsteady, but just enough to take the burden out of the work. The jug always had to be hidden, for it went against the religion of too many to be kept out in the open. Them that objected knew it was there, but as long as it was hidden they could make out like it wasn't. That always tickled me, but it was so.

Papa and Faleecy John and me went over to the barn site early that morning and built up several good fires. Folks would be chilled from riding and would need to get warmed up before commencing to work, and the women would need cook fires. We piled up plenty of wood for the women, and laid planks across the saw-horses for a table for them. Faleecy John and I had already piled the logs handy to the four sides, and we couldn't tell of another thing needful to do.

We get up soon on the ridge, so the wagons commenced coming by good sun-up, and at seven-thirty we laid the foundation logs. It was a proud moment for Faleecy John. Papa made an occasion of it by calling a halt when the logs were down and saying a few words. He called attention to how young Faleecy John was to be getting his start, and how hard he'd worked for it. And said it made us all proud of him on account of it. He said he knew he spoke for every man there, that we all hoped him well. And the men yelled and whistled and called out to Faleecy John. But it just made him duck his head and turn red. Any notice like that flustered him. But you could see he liked it just the same and it made him think well of himself.

We kept at the work steady all morning, and by noon the barn was up ready for the roof. We worked in teams, every team fitting into the work of the next like clock work. One team notched logs, the next dragged them where they were needed, another hefted them into place, and others chipped them out to fit. It went fast that way.

The women fixed a good hot dinner, chattering and jabbering away all the time like a covey of magpies. They were enjoying the company of one another, and sometimes I'd get an earful of what they were saying when I'd pass by. They talked about their kids, who'd got married lately, or died. Who'd been ailing and who'd not. New quilt patterns they'd tried, or recipes for bread and pies. Just women's talk, like it is the world over I reckon, allowing for the changes in circumstances.

Lucibel and Lydie was in the midst of them, mainly directing things since it was more or less their party.

Lydie didn't look like the same woman any more. She was might near plump these days, with a peaceful look on her face. It was plain to see she was proud of Faleecy John and her pride went with her, set all through her body in all its motions. It was in the quiet way she stood with one group of women and talked with them, and then moved on to another group. It was in her voice when she explained how they'd set the tables and put the food on. It was in the turn of her head when she looked over at the men at work. It was a light shining bright inside of her.

A lot of the girls were there, too. Ida Stone and Jolie among them. Ida was a tall girl with brown braids wrapped around her head. Seemed like her hair had got darker, and with it had taken some of the copper of the sun into it. I noticed once when she stood in the sun how it glinted and sheened. And the way she wore it, thick braids pinned around her head, gave her the grace of a queen. Her mouth still dimpled at the corner when she laughed. But she was not a girl to be always laughing. Never one to giggle and carry on, when she laughed it was because something pleased or amused her. And I remember she wore a brown plaid dress that day that just suited her. Gave her skin a warm, rich look against it at the neck

Jolie was as pretty as a picture . . . peaches and cream, that was Jolie. Luscious and plump and pink and white, and to save my life I couldn't help remembering how warm her mouth could be against my own when I looked at her, and wished I could kiss her again, then and there! Faleecy John saw me looking at her and nudged me in the ribs. "Git yer mind on yer work," he teased. "They ain't no time fer courtin' 'til the work's done."

I laughed with him and set to work.

By late afternoon the barn was finished, all but chinking and putting the shingles on. We could do those things later. It was a good, roomy, airy barn. And we were all well pleased with it. We all went inside for the frolicking.

Jethro Taylor had brought his fiddle and Faleecy John had his guitar, along with several others who'd brought theirs. So we rounded up the folks for a few singing games. Old Jethro could call while he fiddled. I led off for the first square with Lucibel, who loved to dance almost better than anything. She was light as a feather on her feet, and as pretty as any girl there. "Balance all an' circle eight," old Jethro bawled, and the frolic got under way.

I never had so much fun. I slipped out with the others for a sip of the jug from time to time, but I wouldn't have needed it. My head was light enough with the music and the dancing. I danced with Jolie and with Ida and with Jenny Clark who'd come with her man some time during the afternoon.

We did Bird in the Cage, Old Black Crow, Brown-eyed Mary and Wet Your Whistle. We'd dance until we were tired and then sit while others took the floor. The dust rose from the trampled ground and the smell of moonshine and smoke and new pine logs blended with the oily smell of the lanterns and the odor of sweaty bodies. You'd think it might be unpleasant, and to some it might. But to me it was heady and fine, and I had the feeling of being drunk on it . . . light and carefree and loving all of it.

Faleecy John played his guitar and called some of the squares for a while, but in time he laid it down to dance with the rest of the folks. I saw him dancing with

Lucibel and they were a sight to see. Him so tall and black and her so little and fair. He was a fine dancer, too. Had a shuffling way of walking through the figures that hardly moved his body above the waist. Like cutting butter with a hot knife, so easy he did it. But when it was swing yore pardner! Man, his pardner really knew she'd been swung! When the set was over Lucibel came to sit by me and she was trembling all over. Said her knees wouldn't hold her up until she'd rested a spell.

We broke up pretty early, around ten o'clock I'd say, for the folks had to drive home, some as far as four or five miles. I looked around for Jolie to put her in Carney's wagon, and I saw him and her mother sitting on the wagon seat waiting in the edge of the trees. But she wasn't around. Of course there's always reasons why a girl would have to disappear for a minute or two. Private reasons. So I didn't look too far.

I walked over to where Ida was collecting her dishes and things and asked if I could help her.

"You can put these things in that basket," she said, and I packed them away as she handed them to me.

"Have a good time?" I asked.

"Oh, a wonderful time, Jeff! I've just loved it!"

"So've I," I said, "you're a good dancer, Ida. I didn't know you were so good."

She laughed a little, and the dimple flashed. Even in the firelight I could see it. "I don't reckon you've ever had a chance to know before."

"That's right," I agreed. I was always comfortable with Ida. There was never any foolishness about her. Nothing to ruffle you and get you disturbed. No pointed and sly remarks, no droopy, knowing looks, no breathless leaning of her curves against you. She had them, same as others. But she kept them to herself. I never felt shy and prickly inside when I was around her.

We finished packing her basket and started walking over to the Turner's wagon — she'd come with them. I saw Jolie and Faleecy John then, crossing the other side of the open space. I told Ida good-bye and went to meet them.

"Here's yer girl," Faleecy John said, and he went on to help Ida in the wagon.

I led Jolie around the corner of the barn where the shadows lay deep and dark, and closed my arms around her. "Just for good night," I said, and she lifted her mouth sweetly. It clung, moist and warm, and as always it pulled me down and down into blind, unreasoning feeling. It was the feeling of being plunged into a whirlpool, of sinking in a circling, circling pool, of being pulled, breathless and drowning down and into the center of some rushing tide of movement. It always left me trembly and weak.

When we drew apart her soft breath fanned across my face. Unmistakably it had the faint, sour odor of moonshine. Surprised, I looked at her. "You been down to the jug?" I said.

She laughed . . . a giggle that broke like a bubble in her throat. "Oh, I didn't take a drink," she said, "jist a teeny little sip. Faleecy John dared me to, and I took just one from his dipper."

"Jolie!"

That was Carney yelling, and I bent for one more quick one before we went dashing across the firelight to the wagon.

Faleecy John and I stood and watched them drive off, the girls turning to wave as they disappeared under the trees. He sighed in a deep breath when they'd gone, and we turned back to the fire. Others were loading into their wagons and we had to make the rounds, saying thanks and good-bye to all. Papa and Lucibel and Lydie were there, too, and when everyone was gone we commenced putting out the fires.

We were in that state of happiness and contentment where talking isn't necessary. Just a word or two now and then we flung at each other. Like when Faleecy John said, "Hit shore was fine," and we all agreed.

Or when Lucibel yawned and stretched and said her feet were worn clean down to the nub. And Lydie smoothed her apron down and said she was right wore out, too.

We walked home across the pasture and left Lydie and Faleecy John at their gate, and then we followed the path up to the house. I remember what a long shadow Papa made going ahead in the rising moonlight, and what a short one Lucibel made. And I remember looking back at my own and chuckling because it hippety-hopped over the dried bushes by the pathside. The moonshine, no doubt, making me silly.

# twenty-one

**W**E HAD the barn chinked and roofed by Christmas, and on New Year's Eve Faleecy John bedded down the stalls for the first time and turned his cows in that night. It wouldn't be long now until spring, and he'd have the full price of his land. He'd done fine with his trapping so far, and already he had four prime red fox pelts to add to what he'd trapped. Everything was working out just like he'd planned.

But then a thing happened that changed it all, and for the first time in my life I saw Papa do what I thought was a bad and wrong thing. An unfair and unjust thing. And I had to stand off and see how bad and wrong it was, not being able to do a thing. For there was no changing him, then or later.

It was early in January, and me and Faleecy John were hauling up wood. It had been unseasonably cold before Christmas and we'd burned a heap of wood in the fireplaces. Thinned down like he was Papa wanted the house hotter than usual, and the fires were never allowed to go out. That takes many a stick of wood. There was plenty, actually, but Papa got fidgety about it and sent us to get more. We had it already sawed and split over in the woods.

We had a load on and were driving into the back lot with it when I saw Carney Turner riding up the front drive. I'd seen him in passing from time to time, but not to speak to since the barn raising. He looked more wizened than ever, sitting there on his horse humped over and knotted against the cold.

Faleecy John was driving and he pulled the team around and commenced pitching off wood. "There's Carney Turner," I said, knowing he'd not seen him yet.

"Where?" and he wheeled around.

"Just went in the house."

Faleecy John stood and looked at the horse hitched to the post, and he ran his tongue over his lips where they were chapped from the raw wind. "Wonder what he wants?" he said after a time.

I started throwing the wood off. "Reckon he could be wanting to make a loan?"

Faleecy John pitched a few logs to the ground and then he stopped and slipped his hands out of his gloves and rubbed at his mouth. "You think yer pa'd let him have it?"

"I dunno. Don't even know whether he's got it to spare."

Faleecy John put his gloves on and fell to work again, and we had the wagon nearly unloaded when Papa came to the door and yelled for us to come. "Both of you," he said, "this concerns the two of you."

The wind bit his words off and blew them at us, but even so they were rough and angry. We looked at each other, not knowing what to make of it. Faleecy John crawled down off the wagon and leaned against a wheel while he built a cigarette. He held the sack out to me and I made myself one. I couldn't help taking note how his hand shook when he lit up.

"You act like you were scared," I kidded, lighting my own.

"I am," he said, taking a long drag. "Skeered to hell an' gone. C'mon. Best git it over."

I followed him into the house. Papa and Carney were sitting one on each side the eating table in the kitchen not saying a word when we went in. Lucibel wasn't around, and I reckoned this was a man's business.

Papa didn't waste time or words. "Faleecy John," he said, "Carney tells me you've been fooling around with his girl."

Well, that hit me right in the stomach and I had to pull up a chair. Faleecy John stayed on his feet. He drew on his cigarette and let the smoke dribble out the corner of his mouth. It seemed like a year before he said anything. "What if I have?" he wanted to know, but he slewed his eyes at me quick-like.

I don't know what I expected him to say. I reckon I knew the minute Papa spoke it was true. I reckon I knew that if Faleecy John wanted her bad enough her being my girl wouldnt' stop him. I reckon it all piled up inside me and I knew that never in all the time Jolie had been my girl had I ever trusted either her or him with one another. In a way it was like something I'd been expecting all along. There wasn't much surprise in it, except my surprise at not being surprised. That startled me and turned my thinking inward.

It started back when we were kids, I thought. Back that day when he kissed her and I fought him over it. Back when he'd said she liked it. And I knew I must have known even then he was right. That she did. Known it and hidden it away, refusing to look at it. I didn't condemn myself for it, for man or boy, a man's what he is, and there's no need to excuse himself. It was part and parcel of the whole that I should have hidden from any knowledge of Faleecy John that made him less than what I wanted him to be. Sitting there, looking backward, I knew that I hadn't fought Faleecy John that day on account of Jolie. It was on account of his being something I wouldn't have him be. I wouldn't let him be disloyal to me. Wouldn't face it. Just like I would walk the rail fence, so scared I was sick, rather than have him go home. I wouldn't turn loose of Faleecy John because I had to have him to make me whole.

I wasn't much of a psychologist, but I knew the core of the whole thing lay inside me. Lay in some dark and hidden loneliness. Some ugly, misshapen fear. Some abyss of uncertainty and insecurity. But I couldn't put my finger on what that was. The best I could do was sense it, let it ripple through me and thread out in a shiver of nerve-ends, in some forewarning or prophecy of disaster. And the feel of it and the taste of it dried out my mouth and put a bitter-almond flavor on my tongue. I felt no anger. Only the sawdust in my mouth.

"You admit it, then?" Papa was saying.

"Yeah."

Papa looked across the table at Carney. "What do you want him to do?"

Carney picked at the frayed rim of his hat and spoke

without looking up. "I want him to do right by my girl."

Faleecy John flicked his cigarette butt in the ash bucket, and his chin jutted when he turned toward the men again. "Now wait a minute," he said, and a slow red crept into his face. Not red from shame, but red from anger. I knew the fire was beginning to burn hot. "Now wait a minute. I want the straight of this. What's happened?"

Carney flared up then. "You'd ort to know what's happened!"

"Well, I don't!"

"She's in the family way, an' she says hit's by you." Carney's mouth was wry and his words were truculent.

I thought of the barn-raising, and Jolie's sip from Faleecy John's dipper of moonshine. And I knew that Faleecy John had sipped from a deeper draught than a jug of moonshine.

Faleecy John grunted. "Humph! I don't believe that! An' I'll not believe it until Jolie says so herself!"

"She told me! Ain't that good enough?"

"No! You bring Jolie an' let her do the tellin!"

Papa spoke up. "That's not necessary, Faleecy John. You admit you've been with the girl. That's all I need to know."

Faleecy John whirled on him. "Well, it's not all I need to know. Not by a long shot! Hit ain't you he's tryin' to make marry her. Hit's me. An' it don't go accordin' to my plans. I've got a right to have it proved!"

Papa looked at his hands a minute and then over at Carney. "I think the boy's right, Carney," he said.

Carney nodded. I'd thought he would make a fuss about it, but he never. Just nodded his head. "I'll bring her," he said.

"We'll wait," Papa said, and Carney went out the door letting it slam shut behind him.

As soon as he'd gone Faleecy John pulled a chair up to the table across from Papa. "Mr. Harbin," he said, and I could tell from the slow way he began he was weighing his words, "Mr. Harbin, I don't believe this story Carney's tellin'. I'm not denyin' I've been with Jolie, an' I'm not denyin' it could be true. But hit don't stand to reason she wouldn't of told me first. Hit jist don't go right."

"Why would he be telling it at all, Faleecy John, if there's no truth in it?"

"I don't know. But I don't believe it for a minute. It could be he's gettin' even fer that fox! He's allus held that agin me. . . . "

Papa brushed his hand across his eyes, and his mouth sagged from tiredness. His face looked gray and drawn. "That's silly, Faleecy John. Men don't do things like that. But the thing I can't understand . . . what I can't overlook is the treachery of the whole thing. The disloyalty! She's been Jeff's girl since they were in the first grade almost, and you've known it. How could you do this to Jeff?"

Faleecy John straightened and he looked over at me. "Oh, that," he said. "How do you feel about it, Jeff?"

I felt a slow, dull burning of anger in me at the audacity of his question. He knew. He knew I'd already examined the whole cloth of the thing, its fabric and texture, and found it rotten. I wanted to mash his face in . . . not for Jolie. Not ever for Jolie. But for knowing, and for being so sure he knew that he dared ask that question.

"Did she like it?" I said, and it turned me cold to say it. It seemed inhuman to me that I could string along with him, right down the path he was leading. I didn't want to. I wanted to feel outraged and betrayed. I wanted to say and do all the noble things an outraged lover should say and do. Threaten him. Lash out at him. Charge him with betrayal. I wanted to feel so much in love with Jolie that the whole inside of me would weep over her loss. But I didn't. I didn't feel any of those things. "Did she like it?" I repeated.

Faleecy John laughed. "She liked it," he said, "I told you that before."

"I know. I didn't listen, did I?"

"No. You didn't listen. But I never thought you would. She's trash, Jeff. I allus knowed it."

"Yes," I said. "I reckon I always knew it, too."

Papa was looking at us strangely, as if we were talking a different language. And we were. He wouldn't ever have understood it.

"You see, Mr. Harbin," Faleecy John said, "that ain't got nothin' to do with it."

"Yes, I see," Papa said, but he didn't. I looked at him and inside of me I was begging him to understand. Not to judge. Not to think I was spineless and cowardly. I was pleading for him to believe in me. To believe that I had to take this my way, and use it or reject it for myself. No one could do it for me.

I think when his eyes met mine and locked with mine for a long look he did understand . . . a little. Enough that his face softened and I saw his eyes go wet. That was good enough for me, and I took a deep breath. None of us said anything more until Carney came back with Jolie.

That was an ugly scene. Jolie's face was splotched and her eyes were swollen from crying and when she talked the tears kept overflowing. Her eyes stayed on the floor the whole time and she talked so low you could hardly hear her. But you couldn't mistake what she said. That was plain enough.

"You're lying," Faleecy John said to her harshly when she stopped. "Why didn't you never name it to me?"

Carney shouted across the table at him then. "You cain't talk like that to my girl! You hear! I'll not have it! Besides, why should she tell you? You wouldn't do nothin' fer that Clark girl. Why would she expect you to do anything fer her?"

Papa stood up and motioned to Carney. "That's enough," he said. "I'll go with Faleecy John to get the license tomorrow. That soon enough?"

Carney said yes.

"I'll not do it!" Faleecy John yelled. "I'll not! You cain't make me!"

"Yes," Papa said soft-like and low, "yes, I can make you! And I will. There's been shotgun weddings in this county before, and there can be another one! Yes, I can make you. Furthermore, Faleecy John," he went on, "you'd better forget that piece of land. When you buy, now, it had better be as far away from here as you can get."

"Papa . . ." It was my own voice struggling with words.

Impatiently he turned to me. "I mean it. I'll not have any more of this. I'll not have him on the place!"

All the defiance went out of Faleecy John and he crumpled before Papa's inflexibility. "Mr. Harbin," he begged, "please, sir!"

"No!" and Papa went out the door, swift and unheeding.

Carney looked at Faleecy John and his face was wiped

of anger. "You reckon he meant it?" he said.

Faleecy John turned on him. "Shore he meant it! An' he'll stick to it, you damned fool. If you was thinkin' to have it easy off of me you made a hell of a mistake. You've ruint ary chancet I'll ever have. You're goin' to lose yore place. That's it, ain't it? An' you couldn't wait fer Jeff to git around to marryin' Jolie in his own good time. You had to cinch somethin' now. An' you thought you seen a easy way to git even with me fer that fox, an' feather yer own nest at the same time. You'd git Jolie married off, an' have nothin' to do but set an' hold yer hands from now on. Oh, I seen through it! From the first. But it ain't goin' to work. Fer I'm endin' up a renter, after all. An' they'll not be room fer you in a rent house!"

He stormed out then and Carney took Jolie away with him. I hadn't said a word to her. The whole thing made me sick.

That night I told Papa what had happened after he left but it didn't make any difference. It was like he'd turned to stone. He said none of it mattered except he was tired of it. He didn't want Faleecy John around any more. He was through trying to help him. Through thinking about him. He was through, didn't I understand? That last he shouted at me.

"Yes sir," I said. I had to believe him. He was through.

Lucibel cried and pled with him. "Mark, it's not like you to be so unfeeling. The boy's just made a mistake. Give him a chance. If you take his piece of land away from him no telling what will happen to him."

"I've said all I'm going to say about it."

Lucibel cried softly for a while, and Papa walked the floor, his hands knotted behind his back. The veins in his neck stood out hard and cord-like and his face was dark and red. I was afraid, but I knew I had to try again.

"Papa," I said, pleading both for his patience with me and for Faleecy John, "Papa, it'll ruin Faleecy John's whole life if you do this. I don't say he oughtn't to marry Jolie. Maybe he ought. But let him have the land. Why, the barn's already built. That's his already. It's not reasonable or right to take it away from him."

"I'll decide about that," he said, and his words were clipped and short. "I'll pay him for the barn."

"Papa . . . " I went on, and he stopped in front of the fire and hovered his hands over the flames. "Faleecy John is just like your own boy, Papa. Just like me. . . . "

"Shut up!" he yelled at me, "shut your fool mouth! I'll have no more of this. I'll not have any more . . . I'll not have any bastards on this place, and that ends it!"

And it did. Papa went with Faleecy John to the county seat the next day and they got the license and Jolie and Faleecy John were married that night. They were married in the rent house, with Papa and Lydie the only witnesses.

Lucibel stood at the window during the time we knew they were being married, her face as white as death and her eyes seeking some lost thing over the ridge. "I can't bear it," she said finally, turning from the window. "I can't bear for Faleecy John to be married to that girl!" And she hunched herself up in a chair by the fire and cried like a little lost child.

The worst of it was there never was any baby. Or maybe that was the best of it, depending on the way you looked at it.

# twenty-two

LIKE I SAID, I wasn't mad with Faleecy John. Nor I wasn't mad with Jolie. Although I knew in reason everybody on the ridge expected me to be. To their way of thinking Faleecy John and Jolie had been false, and it wouldn't be more than natural for me to never speak to either one of them again. I reckon there was plenty that thought I wouldn't.

But there was something inside me knew neither Faleecy John nor Jolie had been false. They'd been themselves . . . what was deepest inside them to be. Anything else would have been false. I'd been the one at fault, ever taking it for granted they'd be any different. In a way they'd been false to me. Sure. But that was mostly because I'd let them be, by expecting them not to be. If that sounds complicated, I'm sorry. It was clear to me at the time, and it did a lot to get me through the bad time after they married.

When Papa decided not to let Faleecy John have the land, all my worry over the whole thing was centered on that fact. It's a queer thing, but true, that I never shed one tear of grief over Jolie, and I can't honestly say that I even missed her company. I was too fearful for Faleecy John. Likely if things had gone on and I'd have married Jolie, I'd have gone all my life thinking I loved her. And maybe I would have. But once her and Faleecy John was married that was all there was to it. She didn't make any difference one way or another to me.

Things were grim around the house the next day. Lucibel was quiet, not talking to Papa or me, going about the work like a ghost. She took it mighty hard, it was plain to see, and it was plain, too, that she faulted Papa for interfering.

And Papa was like a man turned to stone. His face had a gray, papery look, and he couldn't eat. I was afraid he was going to come down sick. After dinner he asked me if I was going down to the rent house. "Not today," I told him.

"Well, when you go," he said, "tell Faleecy John I'll pay him three hundred dollars for the barn, cash money. And he can have the bay mare."

They were packing things to move when I got there the next morning. It took me by surprise. But I might have known Faleecy John wouldn't stay on a day longer than he had to.

Lydie and Jolie were in the kitchen packing dishes and things, but they came in to speak. Neither of them looked very happy. Lydie's mouth was set and harsh-looking, and I couldn't say that I blamed her. She had all but had the world with a fence around it and Jolie had come along and spoiled it for her. It was a sorry disappointment for her, there's no denying, and little reason for her to welcome Jolie with open arms.

Jolie was tired and sulky, her mouth turned down at the corners and her eyes still swollen from crying. I thought when I saw the two of them that hard feelings lay before them, and I didn't envy Faleecy John his place between them.

"You got a place already?" I asked Faleecy John. He was taking down the bed in the fireplace room, and hadn't stopped but to say howdy when I came in.

"Yeah," he said, stacking slats against the wall. "Rented the old Hackberry Spur place."

That set me back on my heels. It fairly took my breath away. "Not back over there!" I said, "you can't do that, Faleecy John!"

"Why not?" he bristled. "That's where I come from, an' I reckon it's good enough to go back to."

"Why didn't you buy? Might have been a little place would have suited you. I thought you were done renting."

He snorted and sat down on the bed springs to make a cigarette. "More fool, me! They wasn't but one place I wanted, an' I'm not aimin' to buy none other. I'll rent."

"I'm sorry about that, Faleecy John," I said, hating it worse than I could put in words. "I tried every way I could to get Papa to change his mind, but it was like talking to a stone wall. I don't know what's got into him."

"I do." The words bit off and hung in the air, and I waited for him to go on. But that was all he said. It was like he had opened the crack of a door, and then slammed it shut, and I knew it wasn't for me to open it again. So I didn't try. I just left it lie.

"Is there anything I can do to help with the moving?" I asked.

"Shore. You kin help me load the heavy stuff in the wagon." And I was glad he hadn't shut me out. I hadn't thought he would, for I knew, and I knew that he knew, that nothing was going to make any difference between us. Nothing was said about it, for it didn't have to be. It was just there, like the two sides of a board.

We commenced loading in the stoves and dressers and things, and it was then I remembered what Papa had told me to tell him. "Papa said he would pay you three hundred dollars for the barn, Faleecy John, and he said for you to take the mare."

He threw his cigarette away and stood watching it smoke in the damp. I didn't know but what his pride would get hackled over it, but when he'd studied it over he said, "That's fair enough. Tell him I'll take it, but I'll pay him fifty dollars for the mare. I don't want nothin' I don't pay fer."

I nodded, thinking I didn't blame him, and Papa wouldn't either.

It took the best part of the day to get them moved, all of us working hard. Several wagonloads they had, and I couldn't help remembering the day they'd moved from Hackberry Spur to the rent house, and how one wagon had held everything they had then, and it not crowded. Reckon Faleecy John thought of the same thing for he grinned at me when we drew up in front of the old cabin. "Goin' to be right smart of a puzzle to figger out where to put all this stuff, ain't it?" he said.

"You're not going to stay here, are you?" I asked. "Not for long?"

"No," he said, crawling down over the wagon wheel. He hitched the team and came back to where I was starting to let down the end gate. "No, I ain't aimin' to stay. Hit's jist 'til I git my bearin's agin. I ain't licked, Jeff. Not by a sight, an' you kin tell yer pa that. I've got another load in my barrel, but I ain't ready to shoot yit. This is jist 'til I git ready."

I was glad to hear that. I couldn't accept his being willing to come back to Hackberry Spur permanently. It wasn't like him. He wouldn't be licked that easy. But it eased my mind to hear him say so. "You're going to be powerfully crowded here," I said.

He looked over the cabin, squinting at it. "Oh, I'll throw up a side room in back fer Ma, an' we'll make out."

Lucibel was waiting for news when I got home that evening, and it was plain she was relieved when I told her Faleecy John wasn't aiming to stay at Hackberry Spur indefinitely. "He's just going to stay on there until he figures out something," I said.

She had cried some more about him going back over there, and Papa had looked a little grimmer, if that was possible. I think even he felt some relieved to know that Faleecy John didn't aim to give up.

"He said he'd take the money for the barn," I told him, "But he wants to pay for the mare."

"That's all right," Papa said, and went on eating his supper. But both of us knew that's the way we'd have done it, had we been in his place.

# twenty-three

TIME PASSED, and life went on, the way it has a way of doing. No matter what happens you've got things that have to be done. Getting up, dressing, eating break-fast, feeding the stock and milking, doing the chores around the place. Little things, maybe, all of them, but even with a heavy heart they've got to be done, and the doing of them eases the heaviness somewhat.

And another thing, we finally got Papa to go to the doctor. He'd been having pains in his arms and legs for some time, and lately we'd noticed the joints of his hands swelling. The doctor said it was rheumatism. I reckon it would be called arthritis, nowadays, but then they hadn't heard of arthritis and it was called plain rheumatism. He told Papa he'd have to stay in out of the weather, favor himself more, and gave him a tonic to take to help his appetite.

The rest of the winter we settled into the regular winter work, and there's never a thing so taut and tense but it slacks some under the passing of time and a regular routine. Lucibel commenced talking and laughing again, and she didn't keep her silence between her and Papa. And even though we knew there were days when the hurting in his joints was bad, the gray, tired look passed from his face with the sound of Lucibel's laugh. Things were almost normal again, except that no more was Faleecy John in and out among us, taking any of the meals he happened in for, helping with the chores, teasing Lucibel, or sitting around the fire of an evening eating apples and popcorn. He left a big gap it's true, but it wasn't one we couldn't bridge with trying. He was missed, but there was still a heap of pleasure among the three of us.

No doubt Lucibel missed him more than any. Papa had cut him off of his own accord, and could handle whatever he felt about it in his own way. I never gave it a thought what he was feeling. Whatever it was, he'd had the making of it. And I could still be with Faleecy John when I so wanted. It was Lucibel his going left the most defenseless. There was no way she could feel but that she'd lost a son, for that's what Faleecy John had been like to her from the start.

Still and all, we made out, and it wasn't too bad a making out. Papa got a young fellow from over close to the Gap to rent, and he and his wife and three younguns moved in. When spring came around we knew he was going to do fine, for he was a good worker and steady. It was a relief to know there wasn't going to be any trouble with a renter for a while, leastways.

We put out more tobacco that spring than common, and more corn, and we bought six new cows. "We're kind of spreading out, aren't we?" I asked Papa one evening.

His face lit up in the old, bright way, and he laid his hand on my shoulder and looked over at Lucibel, like she shared a secret with him. She laughed at the two of us. And Papa said, "Half of everything we make from now on is yours, Jeff. You're a full pardner, now."

I couldn't say a word for the knot in my throat, and my eyes stung with quick water. How good he was, my father. How terribly, terribly good he was, always, to me.

Lucibel saw my eyes and she flicked a salt tear from her own right sudden. "Now we'll have no weeping," she said, making a laugh in her throat. "This is a glad time. This is for pleasure and laughing!"

And we all laughed together, and when we went in the other room she opened the organ and played for us, and Papa and I stood behind her to see the words and sang. If the shadow of Faleecy John stood there with us, no one named it. And the time passed until we went to bed.

When the hot season rolled around in July and August, the revival meetings commenced. The ridge has always set a heap of store by religion in any form, and no matter what denomination favored the revival, everybody on the ridge went and took part.

The White Caps had the first meeting near by. You wouldn't know about the White Caps, I reckon. They'd just begun to settle in these parts, coming from Indiana and Ohio, and before that from Pennsylvania. I've heard they had their beginning across the waters in

Switzerland. Part of a Mennonite group that got dissatisfied under the persecution there and moved to America. They had some beliefs we thought queer in these parts, like the women wearing the little white caps all the time, covering them in winter with black bonnets, and all of them dressing just alike in long-sleeved dresses. And the men never wearing ties, nor none of them holding with the wearing of jewelry of any kind. And they baptized different, too. Face forward in the water, three times. In the early days, back in Pennsylvania, they'd been named the River Brethren on account of it, I'd heard.

But whether we held with them or not, we always went to any of their meetings. Like we did when the Methodist or Baptist people had a meeting. The Harbins were Baptists from way back, good Baptists, holding strict to their own doctrines, yet we'd always allowed that any man's religion was his own entitlement, and we'd given to all and gone to all their meetings. So as a matter of course we went to the White Cap meeting that July.

And that was the start of me talking to Ida. I've not explained, have I, that courting was called talking, on the ridge. A boy and girl didn't go with one another, the way they call it nowadays. They were talking.

The first night of the meeting I was sitting with Lucibel and Papa, well toward the back like we always did, for the meeting always held so long that sometimes Papa got tired and stiff and liked to get up and walk around outside the tent. So we sat near the back so's he could get out without causing any commotion.

I saw Ida when she came. She was with her ma, and I thought she looked uncommon pretty in a white dress with a blue sash tied around her waist. Her hair

was braided around her head like always, and when they
sat down under one of the lanterns the light sort of
made a little crown of her braids, and I noticed how
pretty-shaped her head was, and how slender her neck
came up from her shoulders, holding her head high. It
came over me that I'd like to walk her home when the
meeting was over. For that, too, is the way of boys and
girls on the ridge, and that's the way the talking generally commences.

When the preaching finally let out I told Lucibel I
was going to take Ida and her ma home, and asked Papa
to lead my horse home for me. Seemed like they thought
it was a fine idea, too, and both of them smiled at me.

That was the start, and from then on as long as the
meeting held, I'd go for Ida every evening in the buggy.
For the next day after that night Papa told me to take
the buggy if I wanted, and he and Lucibel would use
the spring wagon. So I'd go for Ida, and sit with her
and then take her home. Nobody could mistake we
were talking, for it was all open and in front of the
whole ridge. I think Ida was proud, and I know I was.

It was along toward the last of the meeting, though,
before I spoke to her. I remember how bright the
moon was, and how cool the August night was, and how
warm Ida's shoulder was against mine in the buggy. I
remember we'd been driving along slow, without talking. Just letting the horse have his head, and both of
us taking in the night, comfortable and easy with each
other, and not needing to talk.

Just before we got to her house I pulled the horse
up and stopped. I wrapped the lines around the whip
socket and then turned to her and took one of her
hands in mine. "Ida," I said, and to this day I can
remember how trembly and weak I felt, "Ida, I'd like

a heap for us to go on like this all our lives. I reckon I've been more of a fool than most, for a longer time, not seeing it all the years I've known you. But it's plain to me now, that whether I saw it or not, I've been feeling it a long time. Likely as long as I've known you."

Without saying anything at first, she took her hand away and then she put both arms around my neck and laid her face against mine. When I kissed her it was like the first time I'd ever kissed any girl at all. Fresh, and clean, and sweet. Nothing yet of passion and heat and clinging closeness. Just tenderness and goodness and love. I would have died for her that minute, or any time since.

When she spoke it was in a soft and low voice. "I've always loved you, Jeff. Right from the start."

"Yes," I said, "you were the one called 'shame' when the others named me a crybaby!"

She laughed. "You weren't a crybaby! Not ever. You were just so much easier hurt and scared than most. I knew that."

I knew it, too, so we left it alone. And went on to talk of the things lovers the world over talk of. Ida did ask what Lucibel and Papa would think, and I told her they'd be pleased. That made her proud.

"We'll have to live with them, Ida," I said.

"I'd not want it any different," she said. "That old house is big enough for us all, and Lucibel and I will get along."

What a mort of pleasure there is to a man when his wife says she'll get along with his mother. And he knows she will. I never doubted but that she would. Because I knew she valued the same things I valued, and the Harbin place and its ways and its life would be as important to her as they were to me.

We were married that September. Neither one of us wanted to wait any longer. We were ready for marriage, although we were barely eighteen. We couldn't see any use waiting for time, and Papa and Lucibel thought it was right we should go ahead, too. Papa was pleased I was marrying young. He said he'd wasted half his life or more. But then he always had to take that back, for if he hadn't of waited he wouldn't of got Lucibel, as she was quick to remind him, and he was quick to agree.

Anyhow, we were married in the front parlor. The same room I was born in, only it was a bedroom then, before the rest of the house was added on. Lucibel wanted us to be married there, and Ida wanted it too. She said she liked the idea of starting out being a Harbin in the Harbin house.

So her and Lucibel worked for days before the wedding, cleaning and polishing things up, and then they cut dozens of late roses from Lucibel's garden and put them all over the room. It looked as pretty as a picture. And so did Ida when she stood up beside me in her new white dress she'd made herself. She held a few of the roses in her hands during the ceremony. I forgot and squeezed her hands when I kissed her afterwards, and she didn't let on, but I saw her wiping the drops of blood where the thorns had stuck when she thought I wasn't looking.

She was a precious treasure, my Ida. She was then, and she is now. And if I've made the thorns stick since, she's kept it from me, like she did then. And I almost missed her! It used to give me the shivers to think of it. Suppose my eyes had not been opened to her. Suppose . . . suppose . . . but she'd always laugh and say quit supposing. Things happen the way they're meant to happen, and you can't gainsay them.

When the ceremony was over and we turned around and I took Ida in my arms, I looked over the top of her head at Faleecy John and Jolie. I'd told Papa I wanted Faleecy John at my wedding and he hadn't argued. I looked over the top of Ida's head and I thanked my lucky stars I'd waited for the things Faleecy John always said were too good to waste. They were. And I'd not wasted them.

# twenty-four

**T**HERE WAS never but one cross between Ida and me. She couldn't abide Faleecy John. Not that she ever tried to come between us. For she never. But she didn't like him, and she didn't make any bones about it.

"He's bad, Jeff," she said, "he's all bad."

"No, Ida," I said, gentle, but knowing just the same. "He's not all bad. Some, yes. Maybe most. But I've seen the good. It's there. But good or bad, you know what it's like between us."

"I know," she said, and her dimple flashed at me when she smiled. But it was a hurt smile that day, and she took my hands and laid her face against them. "Jeff, Jeff," she said, "if I could stand between you and whatever's going to hurt you, I would. You know that, don't you?"

"A woman's so silly," I laughed at her, hugging her close, "what could hurt me now?"

"Nothing," she hurried to say. "Nothing. And anyhow I wouldn't change a thing about you for a million dollars!"

That didn't make sense to me. How was my being myself going to get me hurt? There was just one answer to that, so we made love, even if it was a Sunday and broad daylight at that!

Young Jeff was born at the end of the first year. It was Papa's notion he should be born in the same room as me, so we'd moved the parlor furniture out, and our bedroom furniture in, and from that day to this, it's stayed mine and Ida's room. We just left it that way after Jeffie come.

It was Papa went after Granny, though. As scared as I was, and that was so bad I didn't have good sense, he was might nigh as scared, and we couldn't help but laugh at the two of us shaking our coffee cups in the saucers so bad they rattled while we were waiting. Granny and Lucibel tended to Ida, and they both said she had an easy time. After three or four more I knew they were right. But that first time I didn't reckon there'd ever be another Harbin born. Not if I had to father it and Ida had to birth it!

Granny just whooped when I named it that night. She leaned back and laughed until she had to hold her sides! "Listen to the youngun!" she said. "Jist listen!" And she leaned forward and poked her finger right under my nose. "I'll bet you a purty I'll be back over here to birth another'n before the year's out. I'll bet you!"

And durned if she wasn't right!

Mark came by the end of the second year, and then there was a lull before the third boy put in an appearance around the fourth year. I would of liked to call him Faleecy John, but Ida wouldn't have it. "John," she said, "yes. John's a good, fine name. It's a sound, strong name. But I'll not have any Faleecy tacked onto it."

And that settled it, but I told Faleecy John he was named after him just the same. For in my mind he was.

The year Johnnie was born was the year we commenced building on to the house. Papa was so crippled with rheumatism now that we built him a special room, big and airy and roomy, just off the ell. And we got him a new, wide bed all to himself. He said he slept so restless he didn't want to risk bothering Lucibel. But we all knew it was likely her turning in the night hurt him sometimes.

That was the year, too, the tobacco war started. You've doubtless heard of the time we had in some parts of Kentucky in 1907. It was mostly in the counties farther west of us, but we had a right smart trouble around here. Won't nobody admit it now, and you can't get a livelong soul to say he was ever a night rider. But for all that, most was.

The way it happened was that the bottom just dropped right out of the tobacco market. And most of the growers faulted the buyers. There didn't look to be any way to remedy matters, so the farmers roundabout decided to organize, and they formed themselves into what was called the night riders before long. For they rode at night, warning the buyers, warning those that wouldn't come in with them, spreading fear

through the country and doing some violence in the
end.

Faleecy John was right in the middle of it, of course.
It was just the sort of thing he liked most. He was still
over at the Hackberry Spur place, and while he'd im-
proved it some, he'd never done a lot to it. Raised him
a little tobacco crop, a few acres of corn and the like.
He'd sold off most of his cows, and for all I could tell
was following pretty well in Ben's footsteps. He
hunted a lot, fished when he wanted to, went over to
Lo and Behold of a Saturday night and come back
drunk, and roistered with any woman that would let
him. He'd got himself a name for being wild.

It wasn't what I'd thought he would do. I'd taxed
him with it more than once, when we'd be hunting or
fishing together. For we still hunted and fished, and
sometimes worked together, when I'd take a team and
go over to help him out. He'd always say he was biding
his time. The time wasn't ripe yet. Give him time, he'd
say. But when four years had gone by and he'd not
made any move to better himself I doubted if he ever
would, and figured he was on a downhill road for sure.
It made me sad, and more than halfway mad. For I
knew better than most what he could do if he was so
minded. And I had little patience with his plea for
time. I thought he'd had plenty.

He came over one day in the early fall wanting the
loan of our posthole diggers. Said he was going to
fence a piece of new ground. I was sowing winter
wheat where the tobacco had been cut, but I was glad
to stop a while, for my shoulders ached from the swing
of the heavy bag.

We went down to the tool shed to get the diggers,
and it was there he mentioned the night riders. "We'll

be organizin' here, Jeff," he said, "they ain't no two ways about it. Hit's comin' sure as shootin'. You'll want to come in, I reckon."

"I don't know," I said, leaning up against the wall and pulling out my sack of tobacco. I shook a paper full and handed the sack to him. After I'd lit my cigarette and taken a good drag I went on. "Papa and I've talked of it some, Faleecy John, and we don't see much good can come of it. Not the way they're going at it. If they'd organize and meet with the buyers and try to work something out, it'd be different. But this riding of the country at night, burning and horsewhipping and doing violence . . . it gets out of hand too bad!"

Faleecy John hunkered down on some sacks of feed in the corner. "Well, I'm not sayin' it's goin' at it the right way, but hit looks like the leetle fellers has to do somethin' to protect theirselves. If we don't take a stand some place, they ain't no tellin' what'll happen. You big growers ain't bein' hurt like us leetle uns. You've got a big enough crop it'll take up yer losses."

"We're being hurt just as bad as any little growers," I said, and there was some heat in my words. "Our costs are more than yours. And the volume of the crop doesn't begin to make up our losses. We didn't clear a penny on last year's crop, and we don't expect to this year."

"Yes," Faleecy John said dryly, "but you make it up other ways. Yore wife an' younguns don't go hungry when you don't make on yer tobacco. You kin lose last year an' this year an' next year, an' still git along. But a man like Silas Clark cain't. An' I cain't. An' they's plenty more that cain't. Them's the ones that's bein' hurt. An' it's the big growers like you that won't come in that's helpin' do the hurt."

I could see that side of it. I could see plain enough how it would hurt the whole cause of the farmers for one or two of the biggest ones to hold out and continue selling their tobacco at a loss. In theory the plan of organization and boycott was good. And I was sympathetic to it. But in this country, in which every man is free to decide for himself, you couldn't get all the farmers and growers to work together. There'd always be those who went their own way. And it's always been true that when men band themselves together in rebellion, however just their cause, there is violence and needless destruction. It was true in our own Revolution, when the Sons of Liberty did about as much damage as they did good. And it's been true in every mob rule since. It was true now. The purpose of the night riders was all right. They had a right to stand together and protect themselves. I'd have gone along with them on that. But, like always, they took the law in their own hands, and they tried to compel men to come in with them by a reign of terror, riding far and wide burning barns, horsewhipping growers and farmers that hadn't joined up with them, burning the warehouses where the tobacco was stored. They spread violence and lawlessness and terror over the whole countryside, and I couldn't in conscience have any part in it.

"If you don't come in, Jeff," Faleecy John went on, "they ain't nothin' on earth kin save yore barns, an' you'll likely feel the horsehide on yer own bare skin. I'm jist warnin' you fer yer own good."

"That's a chance we'll have to take," I said. "For my part I'm willing to agree not to sell the tobacco this year. I'd rather burn it myself than to do harm by selling it. I don't know whether Papa would agree to that or not. But if it would help any I'd name it to him."

Faleecy John stood up. "I reckon hit wouldn't do no harm. Could be they'd be pacified if they knowed you wasn't going to sell. But I couldn't say."

I knew then they were already organized, and Faleecy John was one of them. I thought probably he had been sent to feel us out. But that was a thing I couldn't do a thing about.

"Come on in and have a cup of coffee," I said.

"No," he said, hoisting the posthole diggers, "I'd better not. Jist go with me."

"I'd better get back to my sowing," I said, and he went on out of the lot and across the field. I hated to see him go like that, and for a minute I had the old, lost feeling I'd had when I was a child and had watched him going home across that same field. The same little, left-behind feeling. But I shrugged it off and went into the house for a cup of coffee.

We talked about it that night, Papa and me, and I asked him what he thought about not selling our tobacco. I could tell he didn't favor it too much. He was strong against the night riders and didn't want any part of them. But he was fair enough to see the side of the little farmers and he said we'd think about it. He didn't want to make any promises just yet, though.

We didn't have time to think about it any more, though, for they came just as we started stripping. It may be that when they heard we'd started stripping they thought we were going ahead and sell, and I don't know but what that was in Papa's mind. It wasn't in mine. Stripping time came, and it just seemed natural to go ahead. I reckon I had some hope it would be settled by market time and we'd get a fair price after all.

I reckon since you've made your first tobacco crop on the ridge now you know what a chore the whole crop is, and how the stripping after the leaf is dry is about the most tedious part of it. And you know, too, that it can't be done until the tobacco has cured. Once it's cured you have to take advantage of every wet, rainy day that damps down the leaves so they can be handled without tearing in order to get through. It came just such a wet season in October, and we commenced stripping.

We had out ten acres that year, and that was four big barns stacked about five tiers high with tobacco. Row on row of it, as pretty a leaf as was ever grown hereabouts. Good, dark tobacco. Nowadays all you hear is golden burley, and the light tobacco brings the best price. But back then everybody grew the dark leaf, and ours was prime.

We'd gone to bed and been asleep some time when Ida waked me. "Your papa's calling you," she said, nudging me awake. "He's at the door."

I roused up and went to the door. "What is it, Papa?"

He was standing there in his nightshirt, his hair tousled and on end. "It's the night riders," he said. "I heard the horses down the road and I've been watching out the window. They're milling around down at the gate to the drive, now. Looks like they're going to pay us a visit."

"I'll get dressed," I said, and turned back in our room.

Ida was leaning on her elbow, her eyes sleepy and the braids of her hair hanging over her shoulders. "What is it?" she asked.

I knew there wasn't any use lying to her. I hated to scare her, but she'd see through anything but the truth. So I told her. Her face got white, but she didn't say a word. Just crawled out of bed and commenced dressing. "What must we do?" she said, then.

"You and Lucibel and the kids stay out of sight. I

don't think there'll be any danger to any of us person-
ally. They may burn the barns, but you all just stay
inside, no matter what."

"Isn't there something we can do to help?"

"You'll be the biggest help by not being any worry to
us," I said, and she smiled at me. I knew I could count
on her not to get panicky and add to our troubles.

I was scared, I'm not denying. Plenty scared. There'd
been tales of men being beaten to death. Not that I
believed them, but still it could happen. It could happen without the men knowing they were beating a man
that hard. And I didn't relish being horsewhipped at
all. But mostly I was scared for Papa. He was too old
and crippled up to face that sort of thing. I made up
my mind I'd do almost anything to keep them from
touching him.

When I came out in the hall he was there waiting,
dressed and with his hair combed. He saw my gun and
told me to put it down. "We don't want any shooting,"
he said.

"I'm not aiming to lay down to them without defend-
ing myself!" I protested.

"Put your gun down, Jeff," he said again. "What
good is your gun going to do?"

"A heap," I said. "I can stand here at a window and
pick them off like crows if they start anything."

"Your neighbors and your friends?" he said. "Silas
Clark and Faleecy John and the boys from Persimmon
Ridge? Pick them off like crows?"

He was right, of course. I wouldn't have done it, and
he knew it. So I put the gun in the corner.

They rode up to the house and hollered for us to
come out. It was Papa opened the door and stepped out
first. I never saw his six foot two stand any taller, and

it made me reach up as close to it as my five foot eleven could get. I stretched it as far as I could when I followed him onto the porch.

They were masked, of course, but they were quiet enough, sitting their horses in a knotted group under the trees. One of them got off and came towards us. I thought of the women. "Let's go out to the barn," I said quickly. "No use scaring the women folks in the house."

They all got off their horses and tied them to the trees and we walked out to the stock barn in the back lot. No one said a word until we got there. And if it had been anybody but Faleecy John did the talking, nothing might have happened, for they were in a reasonable mood until Papa got his back up. And it was knowing Faleecy John was the leader made him do that. I wondered why they'd let Faleecy John speak for them, when they must of known the bad feeling betwixt him and Papa. For I knew the minute Faleecy John spoke and I saw Papa stiffen, that nothing good was going to come of it.

"We've come peaceable enough, Mr. Harbin," he said, and there was no mistaking Faleecy John's voice, "we just want to know what you're going to do with your tobacco."

"Just what I've always done," Papa said, his voice as unbending as his back.

"You mean sell it?" somebody else said, and I thought it was Zeb Tucker from over at Persimmon Ridge.

"I mean sell it," Papa said.

There was a restless murmur of protest from the group, and then Faleecy John spoke again. "I'm sorry, Mr. Harbin, but we cain't let you do that. We jist cain't. We'll have to take measures."

"You mean burn the barns?"

"Well, yes sir."

"Burn them then, and be damned to you!" Papa shouted, and he lunged at Faleecy John, striking him down short and fast before anybody could move.

Half a dozen men were on them at once, and I waded in quick. It seemed to me like they swarmed all over us. I got in two or three good licks before I went down, but of course we hadn't a chance against them. I saw Papa rolling over and over on the ground, clinched with somebody, but since three men were sitting on me there wasn't much I could do. Papa gave them a lot of trouble and finally somebody clouted him over the head with a stick of wood. He went limp, then.

"Tie 'em up," Faleecy John said, and the men scattered looking for rope. I felt relieved since they hadn't brought any. It didn't look like they'd planned to horsewhip us.

They had me hog-tied hand and foot and lashed to a stall in no time. Then I heard Faleecy John ask one of the men where he got the piece of rope they'd started to use on Papa. "Piece of it was hangin' through a crack in the hayloft," the man said. "I jist give it a yank an' it come on down."

"Find another one," Faleecy John said. "I want this one." And he coiled the rope up and slung it over his shoulder. He came over to me. "I'm sorry, Jeff. But I warned you."

I didn't say anything. There was no use. And they went on out to set the barns.

I went to work on the ropes, but I could tell I wasn't going to be able to do a thing with them. Those knots were tied too good. And I was getting in a frenzy over Papa who was still out cold, hanging there limp as a

wet dishrag. I kept on working, though, and finally
Papa stirred. "You all right," I called over to him.

He didn't answer for a second or two, and I reckoned
he was still dazed. Then he moaned a little and I called
him again.

"I'm all right," he said, then. "But I'm sure tied up
good and proper!"

"So am I."

There was a brightness in the barn that told us
they'd fired the tobacco barns, and we could even hear
the crackle of the flames. Papa groaned and I could see
him struggling again with his ropes.

I reckon we struggled uselessly for about half an
hour, then Ida came running. "Get a knife," I told her
the minute I saw her, "and cut us loose."

She ran back to the house, and in a few minutes we
were free. We started for the barns on the run, Ida
with us. "They've gone," she panted, trying hard to
keep up. "We watched from the kitchen window. I
came to find you as soon as they'd ridden off."

The barns were burning with a bright glare against
the night sky. They'd set all four, and the flames
reached up in a tall smoky column that hung, crackling,
in the air. It was fearsome to see. "Damned fools,"
Papa muttered, "didn't care if the whole place burned,
I reckon. Damned ignorant fools!"

But we soon saw there wasn't any danger of anything
else catching from the barns. It had rained the day
before and the ground was still soaked. But it made
you sick to look at the barns. A year's tobacco crop,
and four good barns, gone to cinders and ashes. There
they were, red and flaming against the sky. Tomorrow
they'd be a heap of smoldering ruins.

I felt the same kind of anger that had risen in Papa.

Reckless, heedless destruction of property. They might have been saved if Papa had talked reasonable with them. But I knew how he felt. There's a pride in a man comes to the top when he's pushed, and though he knows he's hurting nobody but himself, it won't let him knuckle under. Even so, he might of, had it not been for Faleecy John making the terms. But seeing the ruin of the barns I couldn't find it in my heart to fault him none. A man has to do what's in him to do.

We turned our backs on them finally and set out for the house. There was a weariness and an oldness in the set of Papa's shoulders and he rubbed his wrists where they'd been rope-burned. He said his head hurt, too. When I felt it there was a knot the size of a hen egg.

Ida had come on to the house before us and when we got inside her and Lucibel were standing at the kitchen window again watching the barns. They were white and shaky. But not crying. Not those two. They'd cry over foolish little things. Like Jeffie falling out of the tree and breaking his arm. Or Johnnie cutting his first tooth on Granny's silver thimble. Or at Christmas or Papa's birthday, from happiness. They could cry quick enough over things like that. But not when they were scared half to death. Not a tear did they have to waste then. Ida even had the loaded gun setting by the window. Only when I picked it up it wasn't loaded any more. By crackey, that girl had shot all six cartridges!

They looked us over to make sure we were all right, and of course Lucibel found the knot on Papa's head, and there was nothing to do but get a basin of water and bathe the knot and fuss and bother over it. Lucibel was clucking like an old mother hen. "What in the

world made you jump on that fellow?" she scolded.
"You might have been killed! Oh, I could kill them!
I could kill every one of them!"

"Even Faleecy John?" I teased.

"Faleecy John!" she said, wheeling towards me. "Was
Faleecy John in that crowd?"

"That was him Papa lighted into," I said.

She turned back and doused iodine on Papa's head.
He yelled fit to kill. But my time was coming, for Ida
took the bottle and commenced swabbing my cuts and
bruises then. I didn't know but what it hurt worse
than the fight.

By and large it was a pretty full evening, and we
were all worn out. When the women folks finished
with our battle scars we took one last look at the barns,
burned to a low, glowing heap now, and started to bed.
That was when Jeffie came tearing into the kitchen, his
little nightshirt flying in the wind. "Hey, pop," he
yelled, "hey. The barns are on fire! Git you a bucket
of water and come on quick!"

I didn't catch him until he was halfway to the barns,
he was going so fast. And Papa called him the little
fireman for a couple of years after that.

# twenty-five

**T**HE ASHES of the old barns were hardly cold before
we commenced rebuilding them. Papa was in a lather
to get them back up again as quick as possible, so within
the week we'd ordered the lumber and had got to work
cleaning up the charred timbers and ash heaps of the
burning. Papa could hardly look at them without cussing, it made him so mad. But by the time the lumber
was delivered we had the mess cleaned up and were
ready to start to work.

Two of the old barns had been log, and of course we
could have raised log barns in their places. But we
decided on good frame barns for all four. And while
we were at it, we enlarged all of them, making them

higher and roomier, and we hinged side vents for better circulation.

We took a pride in getting those barns back up as quick as we could. And in building them even better than they were. It was like we were flying a banner for the whole country to see. A banner that said the Harbins weren't licked. That you could burn their barns to ashes if you liked. But new and better ones would come up in their stead.

The renter and I worked on them every clear day the rest of the winter, putting in long, hard hours, but having the satisfaction of seeing them rise tall against the land. Papa couldn't help much, but he was out there every day just the same.

Folks stopped to pass the time of day, and we had no knowing which of those that stopped had had a part in the burning. They never let on, the ones that had. All acted as sorry over it as could be, and all acted pleased over the rebuilding. Some pitched in and helped a little, an hour or two at a time, just because they were there, talking. Silas came by like that. And Carney Turner, and some of the Harbin cousins. But not Faleecy John. He didn't come.

I saw him one day over at the mill. It was a Saturday and regular mill day and I'd taken our corn over to be ground. He was there with his. He grinned at me when I rode up and came out to lift the corn off the horse for me. "No hard feelings, Jeff?" he said.

I threw a leg over the horse and got down. "None," I said, tying the horse to the rack, "as far as I'm concerned. But you better stay clear of Papa."

"I've been stayin' clear of him fer several years now," he reminded me.

But there was some resentment in me just the same,

try as hard as I would to be just. "Why in tarnation was it you did the talking that night?" I flared up at him. "If it had been anybody else but you, he might not have taken the stand he did. But you put his back up!"

Faleecy John laughed and shrugged his shoulders. "I dunno. Never thought about it." And then he squinted up at the sky. "Goin' to be good fishin' weather in a day or two," he said, easy and soft, "how about us workin' the beaver hole purty soon?"

I couldn't help but let down and laugh. Nothing fazed him. Nothing changed him. Burn your barns out and then ask you to go fishing with him!

We had an early spring that year, and mild, and it moved on into summer so easy we hardly knew it. Lucibel came down with a chill and fever along in April and we had some anxious days about her. But Ida nursed her well and she was up and around in a week or ten days. Feeling a little wobbly, but wanting to get out in the sun and try her legs. She had a taste for some wild greens, she said. So she took her little basket and set off toward the lower pasture looking for creases (cress to an outlander), wild lettuce, poke sallet and mustard greens.

She was gone a considerable time, but when she came back her basket was full. "I've found the best place for wild greens," she said, "nearly every kind. See, Ida?"

She picked them and washed them and cooked them tender with a piece of smoked meat, and if I do say so myself there's no better eating in the world than the first mess of wild greens in the spring. It must be we get tired of so much meat and potatoes and beans during the winter makes them taste so good. But I've sometimes thought just the color of them has a lot to do with it. Anything green looks mighty fine after the dull drabness of gray skies, gray trees and gray earth. Something that's green, something that's living again, has a mighty appeal after winter. I reckon that's why spring is such a favorite season.

After that Lucibel would go for a mess of greens pretty often. Seemed like we had them to eat every week anyways. And she got stronger and the color came back in her cheeks and her eyes greened up as clear as Little Lost Creek. I don't know as I ever saw her look any prettier than she did that spring and summer. For all she was thirty-eight years old, pushing thirty-nine, she looked might near as pretty and young as Ida.

When the season for wild greens was over she'd got in the habit of getting out in the fields and woods pretty often, and she took to looking for wild-flower settings and ferns to transplant to her garden. She found some mighty pretty ones, too. Unusual and odd-looking, and she was always in high spirits over them. She tended her garden carefully, always had, but she had a new interest in it when she commenced finding different things to put in it. She had roses and lilies and all the old-fashioned flowers, and she put her little new wild flowers along the borders. In the dark and shady places she put her ferns, every kind I ever saw or heard of, and little patches of moss she gathered from rocks and trees. Her garden was a sightly place that year. Papa sat there a lot in the sun. For there was little work he could do any more.

The whole place looked good. Looked good and fine, and I had a feeling of joy over it. The new pastures greened up well, the cows dropped their calves on time, the ewes lambed in season, and we didn't have a bit of blue mold or wild fire in the tobacco beds. Things couldn't have looked any nicer.

And amongst the family things were all right, too. For all he couldn't do much work any more Papa was looking better. He'd filled out some and was stouter. Lucibel I've already mentioned. And Ida was fine, and between babies. I loved the little fellows, but I always hated to see Ida carrying one. She never made any fuss over it, and she was most always well and strong, but the sight of her during those times hurt me. The awkwardness and heaviness of her, when she was usually so fleet and quick. It was like seeing her crippled and maimed. I said so once and she laughed at me. "Silly," she said, "we want a big family, don't we?"

We did. For we'd each been an only child and we didn't want that kind of loneliness for our own. Still, I liked the times between babies the best.

The first thing we knew it was September . . . the golden, winey month of the year. Hazy and warm, with a foretaste of fall. And time to start cutting wood! I got my axe one bright afternoon right after dinner with full intentions to commence. But a man couldn't work on a day like that. It would have been a sin. So I put up the axe and got my gun instead. "Might get a couple of squirrels for supper," I told Ida.

She laughed. "You might!"

I liked the heft of my gun in my hand, and it lay light and easy on my shoulder when I swung it up. The sun was warm on my back and when I went into the edge of the woods a frisky bluejay squawked at me for disturbing him. "I'm not going to bother you," I promised him, and went on. I had squirrels on my mind. A mess of fried squirrel would sure taste good! And I won-

dered if Faleecy John had been hunting yet. He was
nearly always the first to go. I remembered all the
times we'd been together. Once we'd got six apiece,
which was mighty good, even in those days when squirrels were plentiful. And we'd taken mine to Lucibel
and I'd gone home to take the night with Faleecy John
and Lydie had cooked three for supper, and three the
next morning for breakfast. Man, if you've never eat
fried squirrel for breakfast, with plenty of hot biscuits
and cream gravy, you've missed half your life! There's
nothing to compare with it.

I had old Snooper to heel, for the ground was dry
and the leaves were rattly, and I didn't want him scaring the squirrels off with scampering around. And
walking along like that, remembering and feeling good
over the memories, I wasn't surprised to see Faleecy
John of a sudden, standing leaning against a tree in a
little clearing on ahead. It was like I had called him up
out of my memories. He was just standing there, his gun
leaning up against the tree beside him, doing nothing.
Like he was waiting. And I all but called out to him,
when I saw what he was waiting for.

Lucibel came running across the clearing from the
far side of the woods. Came running on light feet,
happy and laughing, her yellow dress flying. And
Faleecy John spread his arms and Lucibel ran right into
them! There was no mistaking it was a safe and familiar
embrace to her. And a happy one. Her face was like a
girl's, lighted with love and shining, and as I stood
rooted and frozen, her arms crept around his neck and
he bent his head over hers. I saw his black head lay
against her yellow one, and I wondered numbly why it
should look so natural. Even as I wondered it was be-

fore me. Faleecy John's black head snuggled on a pillow beside Lucibel's, her hair spread over and around
him, and her face turned so that her mouth touched his
cheek. So long ago, I thought. So long ago! And there
was a quickening of hurt and a queasy sickness ran
through me. It was like having the safe, sure world
shake under my feet! Shake and stop on its axis, bringing ruin and destruction in the stopping. It was every
known, loved thing in my life blighted and deadened.
It was the end of time and my own death.

There was no chance of their seeing me, and auto-
matically I laid my hand on Snooper to keep him from
moving or making a noise. And without shame I stayed
hidden and watched. The bitterness of hemlock was in
my mouth, and the agelessness of ultimate betrayal in
my eyes. This was the deepest depth of grief a man
could reach. A depth so far down there was no bottom
nor end to it. It could only swallow the whole man,
pain and all, and grind him between the knives of its
sharpness. Lucibel and Faleecy John. Lucibel and
Faleecy John. Lucibel and Faleecy John. Lucibel and
Faleecy John. Their names ran together and blurred
in my mind until the sound of them stuck like thorns.
The soft, easy syllables of their names pricked into the
folds of my thoughts, and stabbed there, mercilessly. It
was like I would never be free of them again.

It couldn't have been more than an hour she was
there, all told. They sat under the tree and talked,
laughing together, and Faleecy John's arms were always
around her, her head on his shoulder. Often and again
he bent over her lifted face. If I had hoped to be mis-
taken that hope had to be denied. For there was no
mistaking that gladness and shining love which she

lifted to him. Nor the gentleness and tenderness with which her hands framed his face when she stood to say good-bye.

Even in the midst of the hurt I could remember hearing her say to Granny, "I love him better than life itself." Where had that love gone? Where? And I thought of Papa at home, sitting in the sun, his crippled hands resting on his knees. And I thought of the big, airy room that belonged to him alone. It had gone, I knew, in the twenty years between them. Gone with his aging body and his aching joints and his need for a wide bed to himself. Gone out from some need of her still-young self, to a young, strong, handsome lad. Gone to Faleecy John.

Faleecy John helped her gather some ferns, for it was a gladey place, and ferns and moss grew all around. They laughed while they filled her basket, and stopped time and again to hug and kiss. Like they couldn't get enough. I watched, knowing this was but the repetition of their meetings all spring and summer. I thought likely the first time, when she'd come for wild greens, they'd met by accident. But I knew the rest had been by plan. The rest of the times when she'd come for greens and then for ferns and wild flowers. But come really for Faleecy John.

In time she left, with the gladness still on her, and the shine on her face. She turned back to wave a dozen times before she reached the edge of the woods.

When she had finally gone Faleecy John lifted his arms high above his head in a long, yawning stretch, and he threw his head back and laughed. The good laugh a man has when he's feeling fine and prime. Feeling on top of the world. Feeling all man, big and full of life.

I stepped out of the woods. He stood rooted, and

dropped his arms. For the space of a breath he was startled and scared. It was in his eyes and his bearing, and I could almost smell the fear in him. Then he chuckled. "God, Jeff," he said, "you skeered me. I thought it was yer pa."

Papa he would be scared of. Not me. Not Jeffie.

"I've been watching, Faleecy John," I said, "and I think you've got some explaining to do."

"You seen us?"

I nodded.

"Well," he shrugged, "if you seen us, I don't know as they's anything to explain."

"You know you can't do this, don't you?"

"I *am* doing it," and there was the old, arrogant tilt to his chin.

"No," I said, "you're not."

He laughed then. "But I tell you I am! An' that ain't all, Jeffie, my boy!" He took a couple of steps toward me, jutting his jaw and narrowing his eyes. "An' that ain't all! I'm doin' it, an' I'm gittin' by with it! Fer my time's come at last! I've got Mark Harbin exactly where I want him. I been waitin' an' waitin', jist fer the time when I could hurt him jist like he's hurt me! An' now it's here, an' I'm done waitin'."

"Outside of not selling you the land you wanted when has he ever hurt you?"

"When? All my life, that's all! All my life! You know, don't you, that I'm his kid. You know that I'm yer own brother, I reckon."

I didn't know. I didn't know until that minute, but when he said it I wondered how I could have been so blind. It made so many things clear. Why, he'd always even looked like Papa!

The surprise on my face must have shown for he laughed again. "Why, you never knew, did you? Jeffie, 'til the day you die you'll be as innocent as a newborn babe! How could you help but know? I've knowed sincet the time we got lost in the blowdown an' he takened us home an' had that talk with Lydie. I'd ort to of knowed when Ben commenced to mistreat me. Fer it was his knowin' that made him do that. Hurt me? When hasn't he ever? Me, his own boy, the same as you! You were the one got to go to school, remember? I had to stay back an' work. You got your name on your gun, remember? But he couldn't put mine on my gun. Fer I never had ary name but his'n, an' he knowed it. You got the Harbin place . . . all of it. He wouldn't even spare me thirty acres. I got sent back to Hackberry Spur!"

"You were the cause of that, yourself!"

"No! I'd done no more than he had, but he didn't want to be reminded of it. All I've ever got was the piece that was left. An' I'll tell you another thing you've doubtless missed. He killed Ben Squires. Murdered him in cold blood!"

"No!"

"He done so! I suspicioned it at the time. I never thought fer a minute that rope broke. But I found out fer shore in time. That was the rope Zeb Tucker found in the barn that night. An' I takened it home with me to make sure. Hit hadn't broke. Hit had been cut! No wonder he hid it an' never wanted to see it agin!"

There was a dullness to the pain that knowledge brought. And new understanding. Of why Papa had aged so quickly. Of why he had worried over Ben so much. Of so many things, including Granny's impatience with him. For I knew this, too, was true. That in his agony of mind and weariness of trial, Papa had taken the only way he saw out.

"I'm not faultin' him fer that," Faleecy John went

on, "he done me a favor when he done it. Lord knows
Ben Squires wasn't no more to me than a flea! An' I
would of done jist what Mark Harbin done, had I been
in his shoes, fer Ben was blackmailin' him. Ben knowed
before any of us that I wasn't his'n. An' he was holdin'
out fer some land to keep it quiet from Lucibel. I'd
heared him talkin' to Ma, an' I'd heared her pleadin'
with him. No, I don't fault Mark Harbin none fer
gittin' him outen the way. An' I wouldn't have never
helt it over him if he'd done right by me. I'd have helt
down my natural feelin's of wantin' to share equal with
you. I'd have gone my way, an' been a pride to him an'
you an' all, if he'd played square with me. But he takened the only thing I wanted away, jist as I had it
earned. An' I earned it. You know that, Jeffie."

I said nothing, and he went on. "Well, from then on
I've been aimin' to git even. To git it back on him.
I'm not half Mark Harbin fer nothin', an' he'd ort to
know that! So now I've got the rope, an' I'm goin' to
have his wife, an' they ain't a thing he kin do about it.
Fer if he does I'll turn him in fer murder!"

"No, Faleecy John," I said.

But he was too wound up to listen, and the words
were spewing from his mouth. "Don't you know it's
allus been Lucibel fer me? Allus? From the time I kin
remember?"

And I did know it, of course. And she had loved
him differently, too. I went back down the years and
remembered everything . . . the time he bit her neck
. . . and the birthday cake and the candles. The wish on
the candles. The little gray squirrel muff. Everything
. . . even her tears the night he was being married to
Jolie. They all fitted together now. They made a pattern. Numbly I looked around and thought, this is
where we've come down the years. Every bend and

every turn of them was leading to this gladey place. To this time, this hour, this moment in the sun. Every day's breaking had sped us toward it, and every night's darkening had seen us one day closer. To this second of eternity. This moment of reckoning. It was the pattern of the years, bending and turning, but inevitably coming out here.

"No, Faleecy John," I said again.

"An' I tell you yes! We're goin' away together. An' there's nothin' kin stop us. Nothin'!"

I could see Papa sitting in the sun, unknowing and unaware, happy in his unknowing, facing his old years crippled but strong, with Lucibel there to rub the ache out of his twisted hands, to laugh with him and promise him apple pie for supper. I could see him, then, stripped and robbed, left behind empty and useless, shriveled and old, alone and deadened.

And I could see Lucibel setting the blue dishes on the table, her dress skirts swishing starchily when she moved, her laugh rippling out and filling the room, her voice crooning when she bent over the cradle of the new baby that was named for her. I could see her, then, dragged into age and worn down by Faleecy John's tireless young lusts, burdened with a dishonored grief. For whatever happiness she felt in this hour would be brief, but the years of tortured grief would be endless.

"No!" I said.

"Ain't nothin' goin' to stop me," Faleecy John boasted. "Nothin'!"

But there was. Slowly I raised my gun, and I sighted clean and true between his eyes.

There was an unbelieving look on his face when I raised the gun. A wild, startled, surprised look. But it was only there for a moment, like a swift-blowing cloud passing over the sun. Then he grinned. "You wouldn't,

Jeffie," he said, "you wouldn't!" He didn't even try to reach his gun leaning against the tree.

Slowly I squeezed the trigger, and there wasn't even a tremor along the barrel of the gun as I did so. And the bullet went straight and true and bored a round, black hole between his wild, black eyes.

He crumpled, falling slowly, his knees buckling and then his whole body slanting down. Snooper ran to him, sniffed at him and whimpered a little. When I got there, Faleecy John was dead.

I looked at him lying there, looked long and steady. All of Lydie that had ever been in him was drained away in death. There was nothing left of him now but Mark Harbin. And while I looked at him I couldn't have told whether I loved or hated him the most. Couldn't have told whether I'd ever loved him. Or whether I'd always hated him. All I know is that my shoulders were suddenly light of a load they'd always been bent under. And a galled and sore place in my heart felt healed.

No one ever knew but what it was a hunting accident. I said he raised his head over a down log just as I shot. No one ever knew the difference. No one, that is, but Ida, whom I told different, and told why. And I think Granny knew. For the day he was buried she said the same thing to me she'd said to Papa. "A man does what he has to an' fergits it."

Jeff Harbin
Signed

Witnessed:
Henry E. Giles
Sim Parker
March 6, 1950